A RELIGION CALLED

LOVE

DAVID
TROCK

David Trock

A Religion Called Love

Print ISBN: 978-1-48357-001-3
eBook ISBN: 978-1-48357-002-0

Dedicated to Gene Roddenberry

Religion (n): a set of beliefs concerning the cause, nature, and purpose of things

PART 1

First glimpse

1

PART 2

The investigation

99

PART 3

The Trial

187

PART 4

The Tribulations

231

PART 1

First glimpse

1

Kathryn knew the kids were up to something. The day before, they surprised her at the dismissal bell with an ambush of hugs that got her to laugh so hard she could barely breathe—but this time she was ready. With one eye on the clock, she sat behind her desk at the front of the classroom and quietly tended to her papers. The children inched forward in their seats, anxious to pounce, when Kathryn startled them all—she jumped from behind her desk and rushed after them. They screamed and scattered to all corners of the room.

Kathryn—Ms. James to the kindergartners—took a swipe at Emma's flying ponytail, then she turned to grab Cody and realized, as he slowed and stumbled into her arms, that he was actually *trying* to get caught. He writhed about and protested for everyone to hear, but Kathryn wouldn't let go, and when the other children closed ranks to take a few hugs of their own, Cody held tight to the epicenter of the swarm, wishing it would go on forever. The look in his eyes as he gazed up at Kathryn was as innocent as it was beguiling, and she had no problem with it; she knew exactly how he felt.

A moment of exultant calm followed. Kathryn lowered herself to the floor and sat cross-legged to catch her breath. The children followed her there and gathered around like newborn puppies pressing against the warmth of her. She savored their oddly familiar smells, and it occurred to her as they rolled about with slit-eyed grins and sniffles that that these were *her* children; if she were never to bear a child of her own she would remain happy and whole.

All at once, the loud dismissal bell rang and a new crescendo of shrieks and laughter erupted. The children jumped from the floor and hurried about in all directions before falling in line. Kathryn said a few kind words to settle them down for the day and asked them to gather their coats and lunchboxes. When they were all bundled up and ready to go, she led them outside to a grumbling bus at the curb. Cody was last in line, the last to climb aboard. Kathryn gave him a pat on the behind as he struggled to climb the high steps then followed him in to have a look around. Satisfied that all were safely seated, she nodded to the driver and stepped back.

A grunt of gears followed a puff of smoke. The children leaned toward the curbside and tapped against the windows, mouthing unintelligible farewells in Kathryn's direction. She waved in return and blew a kiss. Cody puckered like a goldfish and pressed his lips to the window, but Kathryn had already turned and started walking back toward the building.

She arrived at her empty classroom once more and sat at her desk to think about life as it was. The room was quiet and cavernous without the children in place, the air still brimming with their enthusiasm, and Kathryn had an idea. From a locked drawer on the left side of her desk, she removed a composition book titled, *A Religion Called Love*, and began to write. It would be her last entry.

* * *

The following morning, all five kindergarten classes were taken by bus to an indoor petting zoo known as the Animal Nursery. The converted warehouse contained dozens of farm animals separated by rail and post fencing. The dirt floor was well groomed and covered with straw. A musky aroma was readily noticeable to the adults but did not seem to bother the children at all. Kathryn handed each of her students a small white paper cone filled with dried food pellets to feed the animals as they wished.

Emma was the first to enter the goat's pen, where she was quickly seized upon by a family of hungry goats. She giggled nervously as they fed directly from the paper cone in her hand. They devoured every last food pellet and the paper cone as well. In a neighboring pen, Cody befriended a hairy llama with long eyelashes and a crooked, buck-toothed smile. He ran a hand over its furry mane and decided that they should be friends. He looked around for Ms. James, but couldn't find her anywhere.

Inside the sheep's pen, a frail little girl named Sarah stumbled forward onto her knees and spilled her entire cone of pellets. Three boys burst out laughing at the sight of it—and when Sarah crawled around and tried to pick up the scattered food pellets, a young ram butted her in the rear and thrust her face-down onto the dirt. Immediately, the boys' laughter intensified, leaving Sarah flat on her belly, humiliated and distraught.

Kathryn sensed the commotion and rushed toward the sheep's pen, where she promptly lifted Sarah from the dirt and carried her out of view. She cradled the crying girl and gently stroked her hair until the tears stopped flowing. It didn't matter to Kathryn that she didn't actually know Sarah, whose teacher was apparently elsewhere; she explained in affectionate terms that young rams are playful and like to make friends that way. Minutes later, she handed Sarah a new paper cone and brought her back to the sheep's pen where, after a moment of discretion, the child forgave the animal.

Throughout the ordeal, the other kindergarten teachers were oblivious to the incident; they stood by the entrance discussing their junior colleague's relaxed attire and absence of makeup, her choice of peasant skirts and open sandals. They shared rumors about Kathryn's personal life, tales that were largely untrue but amusing nonetheless—and they were friendly in person but made sport of her in private, mocking her as sensitive and weak. Only Kathryn's closest friends knew that her inner strength belied all superficial assumptions; she was sensitive, but not weak. She understood the needs of little children, their adaptation to the social pecking order, their quiet trepidation of unannounced immersions into new situations, and their ability to forgive—it seemed to be the reason that Kathryn was so uniquely suited to be a kindergarten teacher; she was a sponge for their emotions, a guardian for their needs. She comforted children in ways that mystified the other teachers. In turn, the children willingly sought her guidance, long before the insoluble barriers of adolescence set in.

At Kathryn's urging, Emma took Sarah's hand and the two girls became fast friends; they entered the henhouse where a warm red light over an incubator drew their attention. Emma cupped a yellow chick in her hands and marveled as it peeped and wriggled about. Sarah stood by, watching with a huge smile on her face. It seemed for the time being that her humiliating incident had long passed. The boys who had tormented her moments earlier found new mischief in the pigpen, where they threw fistfuls of hard food pellets directly at the pigs' heads. Frightened and squealing, the pigs were unable to dodge the sting of the pellets. Cody stared incredulously, hesitant to laugh along with the others.

Mercifully, a giant shadow emerged and a magnificent Irish Wolf-hound ambled into view. The tremendous dog, affectionately known as Falkor, stopped at the center of the petting zoo and allowed the children to pet his wiry coat. Inching about, sniffing the ground for errant food pellets, he shoveled his wet nose into the dirt. Cody was awestruck by the size of the animal—forty inches at the shoulder and nearly seven feet on his hind legs. Emma and Sarah managed to reach through and pet him as well, an experience they would never forget.

The best part of the morning, as the children would later attest, was a spontaneous, live birthing of Holland Lop bunnies, narrated in real time by a thoughtful attendant. Cody held tight to Kathryn's hand during the entire spectacle, a gesture that she didn't seem to mind. She was aware of the boy's needs and the emotions that kept him fastened to her. There was little doubt in her mind that she was equally available to the other students—it was a paradox that grown men had similarly come to learn about Kathryn James: she was at once accessible and unattainable.

Outside in the parking lot, the bus drivers passed the time with odd stories and a smoke, amusing themselves with tales of the road and their dealings with kids over the years—bullies, crybabies, nice kids, shy kids—and every permutation of parent. A nature vs. nurture discussion ensued for half an hour until the doors flew open and the children emerged with broad smiles and souvenirs. Kathryn walked happily among them, immersed in the joyful simplicity of the moment, unaware that her professional character had been called into serious question.

The issue began shortly before Christmas when the pastor's son brought in a shoebox diorama of the nativity scene, a worthy effort for the five year old, with a cotton-ball sky, plastic animal figurines and a tiny cradle at the center. Kathryn had asked him to explain its meaning to the other children then politely asked him to bring it home. A dozen finger paintings of winter landscapes and cutout paper snowflakes adorned the classroom walls that winter, but Kathryn said no to the nativity scene, a decision that did not go unnoticed.

The following week, during a storybook reading about telling the truth, Emma raised her hand and asked if God is always watching. Kathryn hesitated, careful to align her response to the story they had just shared and answered yes, God watches all those who believe. But when asked if *she* believes, Kathryn told the truth.

Hardly a provocateur, Kathryn did not subscribe to any particular religion. She understood the meaning of faith in the lives of others and considered most of the churchgoing people in town to be decent, hardworking people—she merely questioned the origins of their faith and the practice of religion in general. To her way of thinking, she believed in something more remarkable than religion; she believed in people.

But not everyone believed in Kathryn. By the time Easter break came around, the children's paper snowflakes had been replaced by the watercolors of spring, and while the other schoolteachers supervised the dipping of hard boiled eggs into pink and blue dyes, Kathryn brought her class to the botanical gardens. Her children pledged allegiance to one nation indivisible, an omission that got the attention of parents and teachers. Beside the flag were three rules posted at the front of her classroom:

Be nice - show respect for all living things.

Be truthful - treat others fairly.

Be responsible - if you make a mess, clean it up.

Such were the lessons that Kathryn imparted each day to her kindergartners—a simple message of kindness and respect that was genuinely believable. If her five-year-old students understood and accepted it, so should their parents, the adults.

But that didn't happen. Kathryn's three rules were criticized as a slight against the Ten Commandments. When word of her attitude spread, she was snubbed in the teacher's lounge, anonymously harassed online and marginalized by a small but formidable core. At dismissal one Friday afternoon, she found herself surrounded outside the door of her own classroom by a throng of angry parents. Confronted by pointed fingers and accusations, she was forced to field questions from all directions. *What kind of teacher are you? What kind of values are you teaching our children? You're a disgrace to the school!*

Kathryn flinched, thinking an object had been hurled in her direction. The brief misperception tugged at her playful sense of humor—she had nearly smiled but thought better of it. By chance, a security guard was making his rounds and diffused the situation by his mere presence. He strolled past the adults, who nodded politely in unison, and when he was out of sight once more, their angry pitch returned. *Don't put confusing thoughts in their minds! You don't have children of your own, stay away from ours!*

Kathryn tried to assure everyone that her personal beliefs were no threat whatsoever to their children. She insisted that only kindness and fairness and the Golden Rule were emphasized in class—but their anger only escalated. Finally, she said, "I'm going home now." She squeezed through the fray and turned to say one more thing: "By the way, if you're certain that *having* a religion is required to be a good teacher, then my religion is *love*—love for one another—love and respect for all living things. *That* is my religion."

Kathryn walked away from the spectacle that Friday afternoon and made little of it. She ended her week in the usual way, on the top step of her cement porch with a cup of green mint chocolate chip ice cream. A roach clip sat in the porcelain ashtray beside her. "Sugar Magnolia" echoed in her thoughts. A crescent moon lit a corner of the sky that evening and she slept well.

The following day, Kathryn's body was discovered at home with no sign of forced entry—no evidence of rape or robbery. She was only twenty eight when it happened, a crime that roused the neighborhood from its provincial slumber. Neighbors whispered from behind the yellow police tape that she should have been more careful. A patrol car idled silently at the curb with lights running. Curious onlookers gathered to see what was going on, speculating among themselves about the pretty kindergarten teacher inside. Detectives arrived in short order to ask them what they had seen or heard, and their responses were predictably useless. No less than a dozen different stories belied the fact that nobody knew exactly why Kathryn James was dead or who was responsible.

A five-block area was scoured for evidence. Detectives went door to door looking for clues. One reclusive neighbor protested for being questioned more than once, but Detective Robin Noel didn't care; she was accustomed to that kind of response.

2

Pastor Warren stepped up to the pulpit and expressed his most profound sorrow at the crime that was foremost on everyone's minds. He offered condolences to Kathryn's grieving parents, who were not in attendance, and assured his faithful congregants that Kathryn had moved on to a better place. He pointed out the rare opportunity that tragic circumstances offer a grieving community—a chance to reflect upon the love of God, whose purpose may be questioned during such times, but should never be doubted. He said:

"The Lord shall descend from heaven with a shout with the voice of the archangel and with the trump of God, and the dead in Christ shall rise first. Then we who are alive and remain shall be caught up together with them in the clouds, to meet the Lord in the air, and so shall we ever be with the Lord."

He reminded his congregants about the *end of days*—the *rapture* that would divide good from evil: *"The sun will grow dark and the moon will not give its light, and the stars will be falling from heaven, and the powers in the sky will be shaken; and then they will see the Son of Man coming on the clouds with great power and glory. And then he will send forth his angels and he will gather his elect from the four winds, from the end of earth to the end of heaven."*

Nearly two hundred people filed out of church that Sunday morning, stirred by the pastor's venerated words. They paused briefly to share a kind remark and a handshake before heading into the parking lot. Two school teachers greeted each other warmly and agreed to carry on in Kathryn's absence.

The following Monday morning, Cody didn't want to get out of bed. He had complained of a belly ache and pleaded to stay home, but his mother was running late for work and did not have time to get a babysitter. On their way to the bus stop, Cody's mother tugged at his hand to keep them moving. Everything felt wrong that day. A substitute teacher found Kathryn's classroom silent as a tomb. A cryptic announcement over the loud speaker was tinny and garbled and made little sense to the children, who knew that something awful had happened. Though most of them had been insulated from the harsh truth, a few were told the bloody details, and the rest were simply told that Ms. James wouldn't be coming back.

The funeral took place less than a mile from Kathryn's childhood home. Friends and family parked their cars along a narrow lane and stepped over a length of spongy grass to the burial site, where they gathered amidst tearful smiles and hugs of bittersweet reunion. Those who knew Kathryn best were curious to know why she was being interred, fairly certain that she would have preferred to have her body cremated or donated to science. Her grief-stricken parents acknowledged this in principle, explaining that everything had happened so quickly and that Kathryn was too young to leave any instructions.

When a quorum had at last arrived, all discussions ceased. A woman with waves of dark, graying hair stepped forward to identify herself as a humanist celebrant. She made a few introductory comments about Kathryn's life and embarked on a secular service that was perceptibly devoid of biblical reference—there was no inference about heaven or the afterlife, no platitudes about God's greater purpose for Kathryn's death, and certainly no assertion that she was resting in a better place. She said:

"Death has come to our dear friend, Kathryn James, as it comes to all living things. We now find ourselves in Kathryn's absence and look to each other for guidance and comfort. In this way, love and understanding can triumph over pain, which is what she would have wanted.

Let us always remember Kathryn as a unique individual, who gave so much to her precious students. May our memories of Kathryn bring delight to our hearts and strengthen us in times of need. Let us always be grateful for Kathryn's presence in our lives. As living memories, we now possess the greatest gift one person can give to another, to honor her by living peacefully and productively in the days ahead."

Her mother briefly spoke and thanked everyone for being there. Her father, bereft as only a loving father can be, read a sampling of Kathryn's personal musings. He quoted directly from her handwritten manuscript, *"A Religion Called Love,"* to the delight of her friends, who laughed and cried at the warmth of her self-effacing humor. It was during this moment that the tragedy of Kathryn's death was most palpable. Her words were inspirational to those who had never heard such things—she explained that all people, regardless of wealth or personal circumstances, deserve a spiritual vehicle in their lives, a source of hope and comfort without the pretense of worship. She went further to suggest a more sensible faith to unify people of all cultures, and that faith, she asserted, without fear of reprisal, is *love.* Powerful as anything in the scripture, Kathryn insisted that *love* is the force that makes life worth living—the love of a child, the love of country or a dear friend, a team or a beloved pet. She described the *passion* one feels for another, the *eros*, driven by romance and physical attraction, and she wrote about platonic love, the *philia* that reflects one's affection for a friend or a thing. She even included *agape*, the love of God, documented by centuries of worship, the passion driven by religious belief.

After the funeral, a dog-eared copy of *"A Religion Called Love"* was disseminated by Kathryn's dissenters in an effort to ridicule her, but instead the opposite happened—her ideas gained traction that generated widespread discussion and debate. Not even Kathryn would have predicted the irony of a new movement taking form this way, a vehicle for kindness and tolerance that would spread posthumously despite the efforts of a watchful clergy to the contrary.

To be sure, Kathryn James had never thought of herself as a transformative figure, though history would record her as such, and biographers would rummage through the details of her life to make sense of who she was. Her beliefs were secular yet wholly spiritual. Her boundless faith in humanity called attention to the resilient core of human goodness. She regarded miracles and tragedies as random events that occur despite improbable odds and saw no reason to attribute them to a higher purpose. Rather, she cherished the ordinary events of daily life, the precious moments that slip away.

In matters of romance, Kathryn recognized the capricious nature of love—that people willingly expose themselves to hurt but acclimate to the situations that serve them best. People accept the love that's *available* to them. They mourn the loss of love and welcome new love with equal passion, whether the event is a birth, a wedding or a funeral. Kathryn recognized the merits of religious ceremonies during such times, but insisted that a belief in one faith or another had become extraneous in the modern world; the more vital part, she insisted, was the *gathering*—being there, together—to amplify the experience. She admitted that organized religion had long been the chosen vehicle when there were few other resources, but not anymore.

She acknowledged the timeless questions: *What is the meaning of life? What happens after we die? Why do bad things happen to good people?* She freely posed these questions but didn't consume herself with a search for the answers. She found little need to dwell upon the unknowable notions of heaven or hell or the unlikely explanations posed in the scriptures; instead, she embraced the more reasonable aspects of religion, such as peaceful congregation, charity and self-examination, and brought them closer to reality—not with incense but common sense, not with the holy spirit but with the spirit of humanity—to promote prosperity without greed, and good deeds for the sake of good. Kathryn's classroom was an incubator for these ideas. Her students learned to love and respect one another, and thrived by following her example.

Even in her absence.

Standing behind the mourners at the funeral were watchful detectives and curious neighbors whose emotions were held in check by the shock of what had happened. Detective Robin Noel watched carefully for clues, alert to those whose expressions did not quite match the mood of the funeral service. The school principal and most teachers came to pay their respects. Even Kathryn's brazen assailant was there; he stood with the others and bowed his head at the thoughtful words of her remembrance.

The humanist celebrant continued: *"Kathryn wrote in her manuscript that a prayer is a wish and a blessing is a gift, and any deeper meaning would be speculative at best. She believed that happiness comes from within, not from riches or reward, and that a healthy perspective can bring joy to any moment, even in the setting of sickness,*

poverty, or bereavement. In fact, it's the acceptance of life's imperma-
nence, she wrote, that soothes the pain of loss when it inevitably hap-
pens. This is why she referred to life as a roller coaster, not because
of the ups and downs or twists and turns, but because of its limits.
Eventually the ride comes to a halt for everyone, no exceptions, no
repeat rides. How prophetic.

Let me share in closing that Kathryn generously gave to others
and asked for little in return. She brightened the lives of those who
knew her, and we are all better for it. Let us always consider Kathryn's
example and continue to learn from her. There will now be a moment
of silence."

When the last few handfuls of dirt were ceremoniously tossed
onto the casket, the service uneventfully ended. A solemn retreat to
the parking area was followed by a procession of tail lights through
the cemetery gates. Two gravediggers came forward with shovels in
hand to finish the task left for them. As they slashed their blades into
the earth, one man—Dr. Reed Palmer—stood by watching, waiting until they were done, as if Kathryn might still awaken from her
slumber to announce the truth of what had happened.

3

Eventually, Dr. Reed Palmer's staff stopped asking if he was okay—no more patronizing words of comfort, no gentle pat on the hand as they walked away. For them, it was time to move on.

He stood behind the sliding glass that separated Shirley's reception desk from the waiting room and looked through. Three patients sat in comfortable armchairs. Lazy plantings dangled to the floors. A crack of morning sunlight slipped through the blinds and formed a thin line across the wall. At the far corner of the room, a woman reading a fashion magazine looked up and caught the doctor's eye.

The moment was innocent enough. Reed considered the boundaries between them, the soft touch that creates an air of intimacy at first, and for reasons he had not quite figured out, either due to the professional atmosphere or his reserved manner, he assumed the unlikely role of confessor. His patients divulged the most intimate details about their troubled marriages, white collar crimes, sexual escapades and more—and Reed listened without judgment, because in the exam room the promise of confidentiality transcended the secrets he had come to know.

Shirley looked up over the top edge of her glasses. "You have Henry in room one."

Henry Johnson had built his last cabinet in this world and waited to die. The pain in his back was too severe to want another day.

"I'm running out of ideas for him," Reed said.

"You'll think of something—" Before Shirley could say another word, the front door flew open and an unscheduled patient stepped inside, followed by a second patient who had arrived too early, both of them hovering over Shirley's desk, posturing for her attention. Shirley Glick, divorced at forty-three with little formal education, had more common sense than most. She handled the daily barrage of phone calls, calmed the troubled voices, even watered the plants—and when the unexpected overflows and add-ons reached critical mass and it seemed the day would never end, Dr. Palmer would announce to everyone within hearing distance that Shirley was the real boss of the office. Then he would stand back and watch her suppress an exasperated grin to signal that she liked the recognition but not the attention. That look was enough to get him through the day.

His decision to open a community health center surprised the medical school professors, who had expected him to become a cardiologist or a surgeon, but Reed knew exactly what he wanted. His desire to help those in need was fitting for his empathetic nature. Well versed in physiology and pharmacology, he was particularly good at treating chronic pain with the best of allopathic and alternative medicine. Some called it complimentary and others called it integrative medicine. In deference, Dr. Palmer did whatever he felt worked best. He recognized the patterns of behavior that invite poor health, the untoward effects of overeating, insomnia and substance abuse that can overwhelm a body's regulatory mechanisms. With this in mind, he encouraged his patients to adjust their habits and lifestyles to prevent illness, and he did this without being judgmental.

He stood outside exam room number one where Penny was busy setting up the first patient of the day. The muted sound of her voice through the door was strangely comforting. Penny had that effect on people; she lacked Shirley's inveterate skills, though her pale blue eyes and innocent smile brought out the best in others. Always pleasant and approachable, she ignored the advances of unruly men who misperceived her kindness as an opportunity to get to know her better—even when dressed in ridiculous paper gowns with their hairy legs dangling from the exam table, they made suggestive comments that Penny ignored out of naiveté, keeping them befuddled in their compromised positions.

In matters of faith, Penny was a true believer. From the plastic clip that held her blonde ponytail in place to the tips of her white clogs, she believed in The Lord our God and His divine mastery of the universe. At the end of each day, her prayers were ritually followed by a click of the bedside lamp and eight hours of peaceful slumber. In her heart and mind, there was no doubt that Christ was her savior, the living son and embodiment of the Almighty, crucified for the sins of man and resurrected to rule in the Kingdom of Heaven. The lessons she learned in Sunday school were echoed in her daily thoughts and prayers, and the good deeds she performed were but a small part of a life well lived. She was the personification of goodness and took none of the credit. Like Jesus himself, Penny Brant was a shining example of faith at its best, her influence taking shape in human form.

Shirley, on the other hand, was genuinely frank and pragmatic. Openly wary of religious belief or anything as whimsical as faith or prayer, she loved Penny nonetheless, and since the office was busy enough to keep them distracted, religion was a subject the two women easily avoided. They shared something of greater significance, namely a mutual devotion to Dr. Palmer and his patients. It was a recipe that worked well for all three: Penny was the charming ingénue, Shirley the formidable den mother, and both served as unwitting foils for Reed's dry humor. The patients enjoyed the quips and barbs that brought an air of levity to the office.

But if one was feeling unwell or unhappy, the other two became unsettled. When Shirley was rushed to the hospital with a hot gall bladder, Reed shut the office early to join Penny at her bedside. When Penny's mother suffered a fatal heart attack, Reed covered the funeral expenses and helped Shirley with the chapel arrangements. And in the wake of Kathryn's death, Penny and Shirley lightened Reed's schedule and deflected all but the most urgent phone calls.

Penny emerged from the exam room with a look of concern that did not bode well for old Henry inside. Reed prepared himself for the task ahead, the challenge of tapping into something positive, something hopeful. He opened the door with a friendly nod.

Henry pushed himself out of his armchair and took a moment to straighten. Still broad shouldered for a man of seventy-eight, he walked past Reed with the unhurried grace of a country horse. He stopped at the edge of the exam table and took a shaky grip to each side. For a moment it seemed he was too large for the table. Reed extended a hand to keep him from falling, but Henry waved him off. Long accustomed to the imperfect fit of a small world, he did not make a fuss—it wasn't Henry's nature to complain about things he couldn't change. During his years of hard work as a carpenter, the gift of patience came in handy, whether he was searching for the right tool or a solution to a tricky problem. But Henry was running out of time. When the oncologists said they had nothing left to offer, he wished them well and moved on.

Reed rubbed his hands together and tried to purge the doubts that loom when the odds of success are poor. He lifted the back of Henry's shirt to study the topography of his back. The lines and markings that defined him were like the rings of a tree—so many stories to tell. He probed along the edge of his *quadratus lumborum,* the sinewy bands of muscle at the pelvic brim, then leaned forward with the leverage of his own weight and pressed firmly into the surrounding tissues. It seemed he found the spot he was looking for. "Stay right there," he said to Henry.

Reed poked his head out the door and asked Penny to set up a "one & one," their shorthand for a syringe of 1cc triamcinolone and 1cc bupivacaine. She came into the exam room and organized the items on a Mayo stand along with a Betadine stick, two alcohol swabs, a can of ethyl chloride spray, a 4x4 gauze pad, and a latex-free bandage. On cue, she handed each item to Reed in a well-rehearsed manner. He cleaned and prepped the area, sprayed the coolant over the target, and inserted the 25 gauge needle into Henry's right iliolumbar junction. Careful to avoid any major vessels, he injected the admixture and held the sterile gauze in place.

Henry's breathing slowed, his eyelids grew heavy. A rush of distant memories flooded his thoughts, the smell of freshly cut grass, a lawnmower blade whirring, Grace's pot roast simmering on the stove, an oscillating fan in the corner. Caught between past and present, he opened his eyes and touched a corner of his back.

"Maybe you should stay there a while longer," Reed said.

Henry was in no rush to leave. It seemed like yesterday that he was a robust young carpenter who loved to tell everyone about the day he first met his wife. "*I was installing a set of cabinets for her parents when she walked into the room, and that was it for me. I finished the job in the afternoon and returned later on to ask her parents if they were happy with my work. I'm pretty sure they knew why I came back. Grace and I sat on the porch for a while and she asked me to come in for coffee…"*

As newlyweds, Henry and Grace were inseparable; they worked long hours to save for a home, awakened to crying babies who became children with scabbed knees, and then teenagers who stayed out late and worried them sick—and when the nest was empty once more, they found joy and comfort in each other's arms all over again. They shared coffee and played scrabble and drove around looking for antiques and armfuls of presents for their grandchildren, wanting little more than another day together. In the twilight of their lives, their romantic tendencies long cooled, an unspoken devotion kept them afloat. Grace spiraled into the throes of dementia, locked in her own world, and Henry could only hope to survive a bit longer, so she wouldn't have to be afraid or alone.

"Are you okay there?"

"I'm fine," Henry said.

Reed saw the familiar weariness in his eyes, the tired expression of those who are ready to die, a retiring submissiveness near the end. He knew it had been a struggle for Henry, who was running out of time. "Why don't you bring Grace with you next time? I'd like to see her again."

"No, she wouldn't recognize you anymore." His eyes moistened. "Grace, what are you looking at?"

Reed observed without judgment. He helped Henry off the table and escorted him to the waiting room, where they took a moment to say their goodbyes. The grip of their handshake was held a bit longer than usual, both of them knowing. Henry Johnson would die soon, there was no changing that. But his back felt better for the time being—well enough to walk home.

Reed stood by the window and watched Henry disappear beneath a canopy of thick oak leaves, their engorged roots bursting through the concrete sidewalks around them. When did everything change? What happened to the lady who walked her little dog five times a day? Rain or shine, she followed that tiny stick of a dog up and down the curbside until there was nothing left to sniff.

An elderly woman with an aluminum walker clanked her way inside. Penny tapped Reed on the arm. "Next patient in room two."

"Who is it?"

"Bence Jones." She nudged him in the direction of the exam room and left him there.

Reed took the doorknob and waited for the insidious aversion to pass. It was the assistant DA's third visit since Kathryn's death. Reed figured he was sniffing around for clues, though his aversion to Bence had more to do with the fact that they simply did not like each other, not even in high school. He didn't appreciate Bence's queries about personal matters or his attempts to procure information about this or that person in the neighborhood. During his last visit, he off-handedly asked Reed about his whereabouts on the day of Kathryn's murder, an inquiry that both men found unsettling.

With little choice, Reed entered the exam room and found Bence half-naked on the table. They shared a minimalist greeting, after which Bence described a nagging discomfort between his shoulder blades. Reed nodded impassively and moved toward him as one would approach the edge of a cliff, wary of the shrinking space between them. He embarked on a cursory exam and found nothing wrong, just a bit of tension here and there—so he kept one eye on the clock and endured the assistant DA's probing with as much professional equanimity as he could muster.

It seemed that any contact in the wake of Kathryn's death was strained. Neither would deny a mutual resentment fueled by a shared affinity for the same woman, or that Kathryn would have been amused by their silly, competitive meanderings. She would have teased them for involving her at all.

Reed's fingers arrived at the soft tissues at the front of Bence's neck—the vital cartilage just below the hyoid bone—and the juxtaposition amused him. The tiniest squeeze of a thumb could be fatal. He considered Bence to be vulnerable at the precise moment that Bence thought of him as subservient! How different they were, a perfect example of cordial enmity. They were two adversaries stuck in the same small town, at once antagonistic and disparate as the lion and hyena.

When the session finally ended, Reed turned his back on the assistant DA and hovered over the sink to thoroughly wash his hands. He scrubbed vigorously and chided himself for letting Bence get under his skin so easily. How little things had changed. Back in high school, Reed had thought of Bence as a sanctimonious tattletale, destined to become a politician or a televangelist—a public figure that thrives on power and attention by pointing a righteous finger at others, the sinners. Not surprisingly, Bence thought of Reed in equally unflattering terms as a needy attention-grabber and detestable sycophant, always the ingratiating teacher's pet with his hand in the air.

Bence stepped off the exam table, tucked his shirt into his pants and checked his hair in the mirror. Before leaving, he stopped by the front desk to share a few words with Shirley. Reed observed with a pang of uneasiness. He waited until Bence left the office then wandered over to Shirley's side. "What did he want?"

"Nothing really, he asked me how long I've been working here."

"That's all?"

"He told me a few interesting things about the old neighborhood." Shirley grinned. "Penny said you don't like him."

Reed didn't deny it. "We went to high school together."

"Isn't he the lawyer whose wife was raped a few years ago?"

Reed gulped. "That's right."

"I remember because we got our house alarmed right afterwards," Shirley said.

"And they never found the guy."

"It wasn't just one," she added. "The newspapers said three men broke into the house and held him at gunpoint."

A patient in the waiting room looked up. Reed closed the sliding glass partition and lowered his voice. "That's right. But whenever he comes into the office he acts like such an ass, it's hard to feel sorry for him."

"Sorry for him? What about *her*? It's amazing that she stayed in town after something like that. I hear she's supposed to be a nice lady."

Reed marveled at the notion that Bence Jones was actually married to a nice lady.

Shirley recalled the frightening news and the three assailants who were never found. For months, people kept their doors securely locked. Bence and Brenda Jones carried on as best as possible in the wake of the incident, hoping their lives would eventually normalize.

But in Brenda's mind the events of that evening only sharpened. According to the police report, Brenda's hair was still damp from the shower when she felt a draft come through the bedroom doorway. She looked over at Bence lying in bed. "Did you hear something?"

He looked up from his book. "Hear what?"

"I heard a noise downstairs."

"Did you put the alarm on?"

"I thought you did." Brenda heard a faint sound of clicking on the kitchen tiles. "There it is again," she whispered. "I think there's someone in the house."

Bence closed his book and propped himself onto an elbow. The look of concern on Brenda's face prompted him to get up and slip on a pair of pants. "Fine, I'll check it out."

He had barely gotten to the door when a large figure rushed in from the hallway and tackled him to the ground. A second man came into the room and grabbed Brenda around the waist. Her scream was muffled by a hand that firmly covered her mouth. Bence managed to wrestle himself free and swung a fist at his assailant. Then a third man appeared and put a gun to the side of his head—and everything stopped.

"Take what you want," Bence said, breathing heavily, "My wallet is on top of the dresser, my wife's jewelry box is over there..."

The three men signaled to each other. "We know where everything is, counselor." At once, they looked at Brenda.

"You fire that thing and my neighbors will call the cops," Bence said, returning their attention to him. "Just take my wallet and get the hell out."

They didn't seem concerned. Bence briefly looked up into the glare of a lamp and received a sharp fist in the eye. A dizzying burst of light blurred his vision. He brought a palm to his cheek and tucked his face downward to protect himself. The youngest of the three kept the gun in place at the side of his head. "Don't move or this thing might go off."

The oldest turned to Brenda. "Listen carefully. My friend here is going to take his hand away from your mouth." He gestured to his partner. "If you make a sound, your husband gets a bullet in his head." Brenda looked at Bence, whose eye had begun to swell. She nodded willingly and the hand was removed from her mouth.

For an interminable few seconds she stood there on display. Brenda Jones, who had never thought of herself as a sexy woman, could not understand how she had become the center of such a spectacle. Her sloppy brown hair, still moist from the shower, fell about her shoulders. She folded her bare arms and shivered. The contour of her breasts and nipples showed beneath her satin nightgown, rising and falling with each shallow breath.

"You're a pretty lady," said the oldest of the three, whose bumpy ingrown hairs covered the skin of his neck. He placed a hand behind Brenda's head and brought his lips to hers. When she did not return his kiss, he drew back to face her. "Open your mouth honey, we're just getting started."

The words she would never forget.

Brenda sought guidance from Bence, whose eyes would not meet hers. Afraid to disobey, she closed her eyes and parted her lips. A tongue entered her mouth. She held both hands at her sides with all ten fingers rigid and spread apart. From behind, a large man lifted the back of her nightgown, wrapped his arms around her body and cupped his hands over her breasts. Fondled from front and rear, sandwiched between the two strangers, Brenda Jones was immersed in a nightmare that seemed impossible only minutes earlier.

Meanwhile, Bence refused to look up. The men lifted Brenda onto the bed, removed her nightgown and panties, and took turns violating her until they were satisfied. The youngest was given his chance too. By the time the three assailants were out the door, Bence and Brenda Jones were huddled together, tied up and gagged in the closet.

And Shirley would get her alarm system. She returned to her place at the reception desk and tended to a ringing phone. On the wall behind her, a poster of Magritte's famous pipe featured the caption, *"Cesi N'est Pas Une Pipe" (This is Not a Pipe)*. Despite all assumptions to the contrary, it was not a pipe but a *painting*, Magritte's reminder that things are not always as they appear.

4

Father Francis grieved for Kathryn to the point of distraction. How the Lord could take such a lovely young woman made no sense at all; she was bright and innocent, and he might have blamed Kathryn's death for his crisis of faith, had his faith not already been in question.

His thoughts far away, he lagged a full car length behind Sister Margaret's minivan as she neared a stop sign that was dangerously obscured by a low-hanging branch. By the time he saw her red taillights, it was too late. He slammed on the brakes and plowed directly into her rear bumper.

The noise of the crash shook the entire block, including Dr. Reed Palmer's office. Everyone in the waiting room rushed to the windows to find out what had happened. They saw two broken vehicles at the center of the street dripping fluid, stuck together in an unspeakable act. Sister Margaret stumbled out of her minivan rubbing the back of her neck, uttering words she hadn't uttered in a long time—words that nobody on God's green earth should ever hear. Father Francis appeared shaken as he strained to unfasten his seatbelt, an airbag slowly deflating onto his lap.

Reed ran outside to the wreckage where witnesses had already assembled with opinions about who was at fault. Fingers pointed to the skid marks with a hearty consensus that the father should have stopped sooner. Only a few dissenters believed the sister's minivan had stopped too short in front of him. Reed pushed through the fray and took Sister Margaret by the upper arm. The smell of oil and exhaust had begun to thicken around them, so he brought her to a safer distance at the curbside. A patrol car slowed to a crawl with blue and red lights flickering to part the crowd. One policeman with short sleeves and tattooed forearms stepped over the double yellow line to redirect traffic while his more seasoned partner approached the bewildered priest with questions.

Father Frank was ashen white from the dusting of his airbag. Struggling to explain, he placed one hand over the top of his head and pointed with the other hand at the skid marks at the center of the street. A copy of Kathryn's manuscript, *A Religion Called Love,* sat on his passenger seat.

Sister Margaret's hands trembled.

"Come with me," Reed said.

"I'm not going to any damned emergency room. Just get me home."

"I'll drive you home myself," he said. "First let's get you inside to make sure you're okay." He gestured to the senior police officer, who recognized him and nodded in return. They stepped past the muted onlookers to the office building where Margaret was received by Penny. The sister, ordinarily in control of most tense situations, would not admit her anxiety inside a doctor's office. As far as she was concerned, the practice of medicine was cold and antiseptic—a place for healing was the church. She surrendered her coat to Penny, who brought her to the back of the office for a series of cervical spine x-rays. Margaret was receptive to Penny's gentle beneficence, a reminder of her own calling to serve. She noticed a small gold crucifix hanging around Penny's neck and felt a wave of serenity that she could not quite define.

Once the x-rays had been taken, Margaret was brought to a treatment room that was harshly lit and uninvitingly sterile, as she had dreaded. An armchair sat beside an exam table. "You can wait here," Penny said. "The doctor will be in shortly."

From his laptop, Reed scrolled through the digital images, zooming in and out to make sure that nothing was missed. A lateral view showed evidence of cervical straightening, a sign of muscle spasm. The facets and discs looked fine without disruption or misalignment. Reed was equally worried about Father Frank, whose behavior had been increasingly troubling. He glanced through the blinds and noticed that the father's car was in the process of being towed. The crowd had dispersed and Father Frank was nowhere to be seen.

Penny poked her head in. "She's ready for you."

"Thanks, I'll be there in a minute." Reed entered the exam room and noticed that Sister Margaret looked surprisingly thinner without her coat and headdress. The outline of her bra was visible beneath a shear white blouse. Reed averted his gaze and modestly gestured with an open hand to invite her onto the exam table. Margaret rose from the chair and stepped past Reed, feeling inexplicably shy, a reaction likely driven by his. An alluring scent of vanilla soap lingered in her wake, another surprise. Sister Margaret found her place on the crinkly white paper and folded her bare arms. Reed moved behind to wrap a warm blanket over her shoulders. "How's that?"

"Good," she said. "You have a nice touch."

"A nice what?"

"Touch."

"Oh." He smiled. He rested his fingertips over each side of her neck and felt the tension surrounding her muscles.

"A car accident, of all things," she said. "I may need to have a little talk with the father about his driving habits."

Reed sympathized; he had seen his share of patients among the clergy, each with human flaws, and none that he admired more than Father Francis. "I'm sure he feels terrible about what happened."

"He *should* feel terrible driving that way," Margaret said. "Thank God I have a forgiving nature."

Reed heard the words *God* and *forgiving* and dismissed them. After Kathryn's death, he felt nothing resembling forgiveness.

"Let's pray the father's next lapse won't be worse," Margaret added, "like running his car off the road or killing an innocent child, God forbid."

"God forbid." The tone of Reed's voice was unmistakable.

The sister glared as if he were one of her Sunday school pupils. "Are we being sarcastic, doctor?"

"No, not at all..."

"Don't lie to me. Something is bothering you, I can tell."

"I don't know what you're talking about."

"Yes you do." She waited.

Reed could no longer deny it. There was no getting past Sister Margaret, and this was not a good time to try. He wanted to frame his thoughts properly to say the right thing, as if his feelings were clear, but he didn't quite know how to express them. "Have you ever noticed the loss of a loved one, followed by a change in religious belief? I mean, after a tragedy, some people find comfort in faith, and others lose their faith altogether."

"Are you trying to say that Kathryn is gone, and now you're questioning your faith? Is that what you're trying to tell me?"

"It's not an easy question for me to answer. Let's just say the notion of a benevolent God has escaped me lately."

"That's fair enough. You're upset, and you have every right to be, but you must believe in something."

They shared a divergent silence. "I believe in people."

"I believe in people too." Margaret agreed, surrendering none of her own religious beliefs.

"You know what I mean."

"You're referring to Kathryn's manuscript," she said.

The mentioning of Kathryn's name put Reed off balance. He recalled a time in his life when he was more conversant under duress, at least more unyielding. "You know, back in college I thought of myself as an objectivist, can you believe that? I felt invincible, indomitable, and unswerving in my beliefs. I actually admired characters like Roark and Galt. What a jerk I must have been."

"Not you," Margaret replied teasingly.

"It's true. Years later, when I began to care for sick patients, I realized that Rand's passion lacked *compassion*. She had little patience for the weak and foolish. She wouldn't have tolerated many of those who need me."

"Actually, Rand would have suggested that the only reason you help others is to make *yourself* feel better. She believed that every agenda is a selfish one."

"You've read her work."

"A long time ago, I read *The Virtue of Selfishness*." She paused to enjoy a wisp of the past. Right away, it was evident that there was once a younger, more vibrant Margaret—a *Maggie* perhaps. The life in her eyes glowed perceptibly. "The more important distinction," she said, "is that objectivism is merely a point of view, not a religion. It was Rand's personal philosophy—and there's a difference between philosophy and religion: one is a study of the human condition and the other is far more precious. Religion offers hope, a belief that you will never be alone, even during your darkest hour. Ayn Rand was oblivious to this. In fact, she had disdain for those who believe."

Reed didn't disagree. "She was a realist, there's no arguing that. Perhaps her attitude would have softened if she'd had children of her own. I mean, she was formidable and respected, but I wonder if she was ever really loved."

"A woman doesn't have to bear a child to be loved," Margaret said.

"That's not what I meant…"

"Because there are many kinds of love, you know. The love of God for example…"

"Yes, of course."

"But you don't think of me as an expert on the subject."

"I doubt that anyone is," Reed said carefully. "Let's just say there are certain *aspects* of love that you may be less qualified to discuss."

"…such as *making* love?"

"That's right. Sex, marriage, romance…"

Margaret grinned as if the car accident never happened. "I wasn't always a nun, my dear."

Reed could not resist a smile too. "Just what are we talking about?"

The modest nun glanced at the closed door, unaccustomed to bearing herself this way. "Alright, I'll tell you. When I was seventeen I fell in love. He had dark hair and brown eyes, and I discovered that falling in love is everything they say it is—the most magical thing I could have imagined." She allowed the brief sensation. "But after a few short months, our fairytale romance fell apart, and I couldn't understand why. More than anything, I wanted to keep him in my life—so I did everything he asked of me, including a few things I'm not terribly proud of. It seemed the more I gave of myself, the more spiteful and distant he became. Looking back now, I realize now that we were both young and immature, but I truly loved him. I remember praying to God that he would love me back, so we could live happily ever after." A distinct sadness fell over her. "Then one day, during a moment of insipid boredom, he announced that it was over. The first true love of my life was finished with me, just like that."

"What did you do?"

"I was crushed—I wanted to die. Can you believe that?"

Reed didn't answer.

"And it only got worse when I saw him with somebody new, a girl who was much prettier. They looked so happy together. I remember standing like an idiot when they walked right by and ignored me. I felt so small and humiliated; it still makes me cringe when I think about it."

"I'm sorry."

Margaret smiled sadly. "It was the worst moment of my life, no question about it. But something profound happened to me that day. At the peak of my despair, I looked up for a sign... a ray of sunlight broke through the clouds, and I found what I was hoping for. I realized that God wanted me to be happy, that He had a plan for me. He wanted me to have a meaningful life in service to the church."

"I'm happy for you."

She looked at Reed suspiciously. "But you still don't *believe*."

"You found something important, that's what matters."

"There's no need to be patronizing," she said. "If my efforts have been in the service to the Lord, what's wrong with that?"

"Nothing is wrong, except where was the Lord when Kathryn needed him? Why are we alive when she's dead?

"That's not for us to know. Maybe her death will become important in ways we can't yet imagine."

"I doubt it. Anyway I can't stop thinking about what happened to her. I wonder what her last moments were like, if the culprit is someone she knew."

"We may never find out."

"That's not good enough," Reed said. "I want to know what happened and why, and it's killing me that I don't. There's a distinct anger building inside of me. I can feel it in my hands."

"The hands you're about to put around my neck?"

"The very same," he said. "But I promise you're safe with me."

"I always feel safe." Margaret brought a hand to her crucifix and held it there.

Reed observed with interest. "Sometimes I wonder what I'd do if I could get my hands on Kathryn's killer before the police do. I wonder what I'm actually capable of."

"Do you have something in mind?" Margaret posed the question in a clinical, dispassionate way.

Reed sensed the balance shifting. "Nothing specific, just a little old fashioned revenge..."

"But you're the gentlest person I know," she said.

"Don't be so sure."

Margaret tried to understand exactly what Reed meant by that. "Alright then, who are you?"

"I'm like everyone else, that's the problem," he said. "After what happened to Kathryn, I've come to the realization that the human race is inherently cruel. We're born innocent as wolf pups until we discover our true predatory nature."

"Really, which one of us is predatory?"

"Both of us," he said. "Don't look so surprised, you should have seen yourself a few minutes ago—you wanted to strangle the good father."

Margaret put on a civilized air. "There are times when a little anger is appropriate."

"All we are is a result of what we have thought."

- Buddha *(563 BC - 483 BC)*

5

Reed cradled Kathryn's body and touched his lips to hers. *Better leave before they come.* He rested her shoulders to the floor and got ready to leave, but he could barely move. A distinct heaviness settled in his feet; it anchored him to the ground and held him in place. The notion of calling the police occurred to him. Finally, his survival instincts kicked in and he left her house through the front door.

* * *

The memory of her lifeless body was indelible; it surfaced on a regular basis. Reed stood in front of an open refrigerator door and stared at a plate of leftovers—yesterday's chicken cutlet parmigiana and spaghetti, even better the second day. He lowered the plate of food into the microwave and watched mindlessly as the carousel turned and the cutlets bubbled up. A vague sensation expanded inside of him, a visceral emptiness that caught him off guard. His body felt like a gyroscope spinning too slowly to keep its balance. His mind was imbued with snapshots of the past—Kathryn's hazel eyes, her light brown hair, images that eclipsed the present with imposing efficiency. *Obsessive love* the experts would call it, not the real thing but something darker—Edvardian love, introspective love—the kind of solitary love he had come to know.

When the beep sounded, he carried his plate to the kitchen table and ate in concert to the hum of the refrigerator and the ticking of the wall clock—the sounds of solitude. He briefly raised the sharp knife to examine its gleaming edge then lowered it onto the soft part of his wrist, where he allowed it to rest. A morbid sensation summoned his curiosity. The word *anomie* sprang to mind, his inability to feel pleasure, its derivation sounding like *without me,* as if he weren't there. Returning the knife to his food, a different word sprang to mind, *anhedonia*—the opposite of hedonism—suggesting not only his absence of pleasure but a *lack of capacity* to experience it. When Kathryn died she took everything.

He went upstairs to wash up, unbuttoning his shirt along the way. A white pedestal sink at the center of the master bathroom had been meticulously cleaned earlier in the day by the nice lady who came on Thursdays. Reed leaned over the sink, splashed a handful of water onto his face, and watched the wetness drip off his chin. He raised a hand to the top of his head and felt nothing. His hair felt like a hat, like someone else's hair. A distinct presence kept him in place; it hovered behind him and beckoned, like a puff of air or a tap on the shoulder, the kind of insipid awareness that is impossible to ignore.

He wandered to the bedroom, dropped his pants to the floor and fell into bed. Flipping through several channels, he settled on a show about extreme animal attacks that featured a crocodile about to lunge from the water, snatch a young wildebeest, and drag it under for a death roll. Another belly filled, another helpless mother watching from the shore.

Reed wondered if anyone could presume to understand her loss. He knew nothing about the maternal grief of a wildebeest or the crocodile's right to survive, yet he was certain that Kathryn's death affected him more intensely than anyone. Had things turned out differently, he imagined that she could have become his wife, perhaps the mother of his children. That his own parents had an idyllic marriage was not irrelevant—they enjoyed an enduring romance and playfully blamed each other for any mishap. Yet there was a darker side to his parent's happiness that belied his own. When Reed was old enough to realize that their love was directed solely at each other, a pit of loneliness grew inside his young heart. He felt unwanted and isolated for reasons that were unclear at the time, with a vague yearning for intimacy that followed him into adulthood. Ordinarily, the outcome of such insidious neglect would be difficult to predict. One can become an incubator of rage or depression—it's a matter of misery turned outward versus inward. Given these two possibilities, Reed chose neither. Instead, a distinct calmness befell him, a calling to serve.

As the credits rolled, he fell into a deep sleep. A host of violent images mixed strangely with the day's tepid events. A leg kicked in vain as an angry mob closed in. At sunrise, he awakened to find Kathryn standing by the light of the curtains, already showered and dressed for the day. The tips of her wet hair touched the back of her shoulders, and Reed marveled at her appearance; she was a phantasm, a silhouette in the morning light, her presence barely perceptible to his morning eyes.

6

Shirley wiped the crumbs from the table and tossed the wet sponge into the sink. "It's not easy finding the right man," she said to Penny. "You think all the pieces will fall into place and everyone will live happily ever after, but it never works out that way. When I was your age, the only thing I wanted was a nice normal family—you know the kind that talks to each other, maybe eats dinner together once in a while?" She restored the chairs to their proper order and stepped back. "So what happens? My husband left me for a woman half my age, my nineteen year old moved in with her boyfriend, and I'm alone all over again."

A crack in her armor showed. Penny took her hand and held it affectionately. Shirley allowed the nurturing gesture. "The funny thing is, when my husband left, I figured it was my fault, like I deserved to be alone."

Reed stepped into the lounge. "You're not alone," he said, cozying up to Shirley. "In fact, I've been meaning to tell you about the feelings I've had for you lately."

"Fuck you." She elbowed him in the ribs and pushed herself away.

Penny smiled uneasily. "You're both sick."

The two converged around Penny and trapped her in a friendly squeeze. When she finally wiggled free, they all returned to the front of the office and found the waiting room buzzing again with patients.

A distressed furniture mover shuffled in utter agony. Moments earlier, he had tried to hoist a heavy mahogany dresser an instant before his partner was ready and felt a sudden snap in his back. Struggling now to stand upright with his partner hanging on to him, each breath was accompanied by a gasp.

"Maybe we should take him first," Penny whispered to Reed.

The hint of pizza on her breath was strangely appealing. "Give him a chance to relax," he said. "He'll be okay." And it was true. The furniture mover would be just fine. When Reed said *he'll be okay*, his staff trusted him, and he came to trust his own instincts as well—instincts that had evolved over time into experience. Knowing when to reassure a patient was a skill that didn't happen overnight; it took years to develop a knack for detecting the warning signs amidst the fog of complaints. And still, he couldn't help but wonder at the end of each day what he might have missed. Whose back pain was actually a symptom of pancreatic cancer or an expanding abdominal aortic aneurysm? Whose elevated blood pressure was a warning sign of renal artery stenosis? Mindful of this, Reed remained humble. He was considered one of the smartest guys in town, yet he was certain that the brightest mind he'd ever known belonged to his oldest friend, Howell Martin.

Howell once told him, "There's only one kind of genius: the kind that creates something from nothing. The genius ignores all precedent, wastes little time deconstructing theory, and quietly replaces the old with the new." So it was with Howell Martin, who answered life's most challenging questions with more questions; yet somewhere along the line it became clear to all who knew Howell that he existed on a different plane, destined to fly on his own.

After high school, Howell found his share of trouble at local bars, where he fell into the dangerous habit of toying with strangers. After a few drinks, he would pontificate about the subtleties of pre-science vs. clairvoyance, or the derivation of the word conscience: *with* science or *against* it? His trademark soliloquies began with inane questions such as *do pretty women smell better*? His unlikely tangents and flights of ideas bordered on insanity, his sharp wit and audacity on a level that essentially fit in nowhere, so Howell spent most of his time alone. Other than Reed, his only real friend was Kathryn.

The three spent many summer evenings on Kathryn's porch, the gray cement porch with black wrought iron railings, where the hours slipped away. As a matter of habit, Kathryn sat on the top step between the two young men who were mindful of her proximity, yet respectful of her boundaries. Their good-natured jousting was friendly on the surface and inevitably became a match of wits. Depending on the mood of the day, Howell steered the conversation toward a tangent of his choosing to show off his cerebral dexterity. Once he raised the topic of *ontology*, a branch of metaphysics that deals with the nature of existence, and proclaimed there's no *opposite* of ontology, no study of the *lack* of existence, which is why he refused to dismiss the possibility of anything. He brought a similar brand of convoluted optimism to most discussions, and Reed and Kathryn were happy to partake.

They were a triumvirate to be reckoned with: three idealistic misfits who had mistakenly found each other. They cherished the warm summer evenings and talked about how to make the world a better place. It was during these impromptu discussions, when the sun was setting and the mood was relaxed, that Kathryn's responses were most valued, and the boys honed the art of listening. Their collective view of the world had expanded beyond their small town. They searched for answers that had eluded so many others, expecting their friendship to endure and bring happiness and security to the unknown. Little did they know that the future was a house of cards; Kathryn's death quietly loomed, and nothing could have prepared them for what was about to happen.

But for a while they were alive. They sat on Kathryn's porch, a private oasis on which she could be shared. The boys' unspoken feelings for her were powerful beyond words—it was difficult to say who loved her more—and their reverie transcended mere lust; they truly admired her. Each considered the possibility that Kathryn might choose one of them someday, and they equally dreaded the prospect. The thought of being the odd man out was excruciating. Given the opportunity, Reed and Howell would have been content to share Kathryn for an eternity.

But there would be no eternity. After the funeral, the boys went their separate ways. One was barely able to face the other. Neither was equipped to deal with Kathryn's loss or the investigation that followed. In the months ahead, Reed tended to his patients while Howell grew isolated to the point of seclusion. To describe them as bereft would have missed the target by a mile; they were completely lost, trapped like birds in an oil slick.

"*I went to medical school because I wanted to ask the big questions. Do we have a soul? Does God exist? What happens after death? And so I gradually moved in the direction of what I can only call a secular spirituality.*"

- Deepak Chopra

7

Early in medical school, Reed discovered that the subject of gross anatomy is not likely to change very much. What had been known for hundreds of years remained at the core of every medical school curriculum—same brachial plexus, same appendix—even the Latin intonation endured. After all, what more is there to know about gross anatomy? Is there a bodily tissue that has not been seen or held or named? And yet, despite its ostensible limits, he felt the study of gross anatomy was essential to understanding everything else, even the gray matter so vital to the human condition, the stuff of dreams and beliefs that had puzzled generations of experts in behavior and theology. For this reason, Reed felt a quiet sense of reverence for his cadaver.

At last, when the cramming of gross anatomy, organic chemistry, physiology, pharmacology, the third year clerkships and fourth year electives had finally come to an end, Reed hoped the cruelty of the process would at least confer a minimum of expertise—but the cruelest joke of all, when the degree of medical doctor had been conferred, was the realization that graduation day was just the calm before the storm. A mere moment of satisfaction was permitted before internship began, and he was thrust back into the pit of futility all over again.

During his absence, Reed had expected Howell to exploit the opportunity to spend time alone with Kathryn, but it didn't work out that way. She said it wouldn't be the same without all three—so they went their separate ways, forged their respective careers and made little contact.

Three years later, with internship and residency securely behind him, Reed could have taken his credentials anywhere. He wouldn't admit or acknowledge Kathryn's lure, though the fact that she had remained unmarried made his decision easy. When Howell heard the news that Reed was coming back, he had mixed feelings, a pang of jealousy perhaps, yet more than anything he looked forward to a renewed proximity to Kathryn. His research was going well; he'd published several key articles on the emerging topic of somatic cell nuclear transfer, and he wanted to share the good news.

The three friends met on Kathryn's porch, where she found her place on the top step between the two young men. Howell brought them up to speed about the details of his ongoing research, described by experts in the field as *promising*. The enthusiasm in his voice was infectious. Kathryn was happy for him, and impressed that he had made progress in a science that was already complicated.

Then it was Reed's turn. He shared stories that were gratifying one moment and dehumanizing the next, and though he was relieved to have a grueling internship and residency behind him, he knew that a lifetime of learning had just begun. Kathryn was impressed with his equanimity and the poise that brought an air of maturity beyond his years. Howell wasn't nearly as impressed.

Finally, it was Kathryn's turn to hold court. She described her lively kindergartners and her exciting role as their teacher. She imitated the games they loved to play, the lessons they had learned, and it was clear that she was happy to be part of their lives. Reed and

Howell envied the five-year-olds who had managed to hijack her attention.

As Kathryn spoke, the boys took turns stealing glances in her direction. They found it difficult to look directly at her, yet they could barely look away. With each furtive glance, they detected new details in her appearance, subtleties that had previously eluded them. There was no question that she was lovely as ever. Her hair was cut an inch shorter. Her toenails were painted an uncommon shade of blue. She had neared the completion of a manuscript titled, *A Religion Called Love*, which she described as an intertwining of love and faith.

On a whim, she asked Reed and Howell if they think it's more important to love *others* or to *be* loved. They glanced at one another, thinking the same thing: which answer would she prefer? On the surface it seemed like a trivial exercise, but they knew it was much more. A chance to validate Kathryn's opinion and gain her favor would allow the victor to watch the other squirm in defeat. They knew from similar jousting in the past that an advantage came not from rushing in with an opinion but to wait for a strong finish. It was a form of intellectual judo that invited the aggressor to commit himself and risk ruin. They also recognized an opportunity to swing at the first pitch and hit the ball out of the park.

Howell was first to speak. "I think it's more important to love others than to *be* loved." He paused. "If more people loved others, the world would be a better place."

Reed glanced in Kathryn's direction, hoping to see a sideways grin or a rolling of the eyes, but her expression showed neither. So he remained silent; better to wait and be asked, then he could watch Howell sink into his shirt collar.

Howell turned to Reed. "What do *you* think?"

"You always do that," Reed said.

"Do what?"

"Ask me what I think. You don't care what I think; you want to know if I *agree*."

"It's the same thing."

"No it's not. You should ask me if I *agree* if that's what you want to know."

"Alright the two of you," Kathryn said. She turned to Reed and asked for his opinion.

Reed pretended to contemplate. "I have to say there's no difference between loving others and *being* loved. They're both love; that's the most important thing."

Kathryn smiled. "Love is always the most important thing," she said.

Reed soaked it up. "Maybe if more people felt that way, there would be less war."

Howell shook his head, anxious to challenge Reed. "You don't know what you're talking about. Wars are fought between nations, and nations are defined by cultural differences. It has nothing to do with love or the lack of it."

"That doesn't mean I'm wrong," Reed said. "You say nations are defined by cultural differences and I say people more *alike* than different. Who's to say which is right?"

"It's not a matter of who's right," Howell said. "Cultural differences offer pride and meaning to otherwise pedestrian lives. Cultures are defined by differences, not similarities."

"You're right about that," Kathryn said. "There *are* differences between *cultures*—but *people* are the same everywhere, regardless of language or religion. And *love* is the same everywhere on the planet."

"I wish I could agree," Howell said. "Unfortunately, *love* is not a global concept. It exists between *individuals*, not between nations, and certainly not between religions."

"Then why can't their religion be *love*?" she mused.

Reed smiled at the thought.

"That's totally unrealistic," Howell said, bothered by Reed's look of approval. "Do you think the Israelis and Palestinians will suddenly love each other someday because they worship the same God?"

"I doubt it," Reed said. "But then, religion has never been helpful in matters of diplomacy. Peace will occur in the Middle East when religion is *removed* from the equation, when people of good conscience realize that their primeval beliefs can be replaced with something better. Think about it, throughout recorded history every civilization known to man has gone from one phase of worship to the next, so what makes you think the current norm is here to stay? Is there a single remnant of Egyptian society that prays to birdlike gods? Where are the ancient Greeks and Romans who were inspired by their mythological heroes? They're all dead and buried, of course. And if those gods are obsolete then what makes the status quo any different? Surely the Roman Empire didn't anticipate the demise of their heroes and neither do we."

"I'm not sure what you're getting at," Howell said.

"He's trying to say that religion, as we know it, has developed in the blink of an eye," Kathryn said in Reed's defense. "Only a few thousand years have ushered in the notion of a single God, a notion that's subjugated as many minds as it's helped. I think we can do better."

Howell spit his gum into the bushes. "And who's going to change the minds of billions—is that supposed to be you?"

"No, of course not," Kathryn said.

"So what are you saying?"

"I'm not sure." She looked away, her mood perceptibly changed.

Reed observed with concern. "Kathryn, are you okay?" He shifted an accusing eye at Howell.

"I'm fine," she said.

Howell said nothing further. In an uncharacteristic display, he backed off.

8

A month before Kathryn's death, Howell Martin was scheduled to deliver a plenary session to members of the National Academy of Science, a forty minute discussion about his ongoing research of somatic cell nuclear transfer. If his findings were correct, he could accelerate the method of tissue harvesting and revolutionize the availability of healthy organs for transplant.

He was admittedly vexed by theoretical concepts such as dark matter and gravitational lensing, though he had little difficulty grasping the fundamentals of human flesh. It was the measure-able substance of human life that made perfect sense to Dr. Howell Martin, who mastered the intricacies of somatic cell nuclear transfer, but didn't know how to get Kathryn James to love him.

Reed had heard about the lecture and did not want to miss any of it. Eager to surprise his friend afterward, he slipped into the lecture hall and sat in the back row. He'd been to several of Howell's presentations and knew what to expect: a volley of opening remarks to introduce the subject, followed by an eclectic mix of pop trivia and hard science to lighten things up. The best part, as Reed had come to learn, was Howell's ability to keep a straight face while making the audience laugh—but this time the mood of the lecture hall was decidedly subdued.

An uneasy silence followed as Howell took his place at the podium. He took a sip of water, adjusted the microphone and uttered a few comments about the unmet needs of society. Then a strange thing happened: Howell's practiced crescendos and dramatic pauses fell flat, his slides were out of order, and it became frighteningly clear at the most inopportune time of Howell's life—the podium at the Academy of Science of all places—that he was faltering. It was a sobering experience for the young scholar, who had been unaccustomed to failure.

Two professors gathered their overcoats and obstructed the light of the projector as they shuffled toward the aisle. Howell noticed but was undeterred; he believed wholeheartedly in his findings and desperately wanted to convince everyone that he was right. Scattered about were bearded professors and jittery colleagues who had grown restless and weary. By the end of Howell's forty-minute lecture, nearly half the original audience had disappeared. Four years of hard work were met with scant applause, and it appeared that Howell Martin was stuck in the starting gate of greatness, destined to remain anonymous.

When the overhead lights were raised once more, an unenthusiastic migration to the exit ensued. A graduate student stepped past an elderly professor emeritus who had apparently fallen asleep. Reed made his way against the current to the podium to offer congratulations, but Howell didn't want to hear it. He powered down and folded his laptop. "What the hell are you doing here?"

"Kathryn said you were lecturing."

"She's here?"

"No, she's at work."

"Oh." Howell rolled up the power cord and stuffed it into a carrying case. "I don't know what it's going to take to get through to them."

"Forget about them; let's get out of here."

"Kathryn told you about the lecture?"

Reed nodded.

Howell glanced at the empty seats. "What the hell, I'm just about out of time anyway."

9

Reed stepped outside to the rear of the office, where Shirley was leaning up against the building, smoking a cigarette. She took a final drag and tossed the rest to the ground. "There, I put it out. Are you happy?"

"I'm always happy."

"The hell you are." She watched him linger in the cloud of smoke and smirked. "Maybe you should start smoking again."

"So I can turn into a pariah like you?"

"I'm not the only one out here," she said.

Reed stared at the cigarette butt on the ground. "You know, in the old days, a man held a cigarette between his thumb and middle finger with the glowing part facing his palm." He imitated the proper technique.

"I can see you've given this a lot of thought."

The afternoon sun hovered above the building and carved a wedge of shade at their feet. At the base of the wall were potted plants arched upwards toward the sky—hearty zebra plants, begonias in red clay pots, jade cacti and other succulents—all slightly tilted in the same direction. Shirley watered and fed them every day with a maternal quality she would deny in an instant. She opened the sliding door halfway and stopped before heading back inside. "By the way, how's your friend the assistant DA?"

"He said his back's still bothering him. It's the same thing every time. I can never find anything wrong." Reed looked at his palms. "He asks so many questions."

"He asked me about you," Shirley said.

"About me?" Reed asked with more curiosity than concern. "What did he want to know?"

"He asked me where you were last weekend."

"Did you tell him?"

"I guess so. It seemed innocent enough."

A wisp of wind chased a family of birds from the trees to the sky. Reed followed Shirley inside and closed the sliding glass door behind them.

* * *

Penny poked her head in. "Do you have a minute?"

"Sure, come in." Reed pushed himself away from the desk and dropped his pen onto a pile of forms.

"If you're busy I can come back."

"No, this is fine." He gestured across the desk for Penny to have a seat. She shut the door and sat on the opposite side of the desk. The formality felt wrong, so Reed walked around the desk to sit in the chair next to hers, and when she crossed her legs and brought a hand to the hem of her skirt, Reed wondered if his eyes had wandered there. "What's on your mind?"

"Nothing really," she said. Her response was credible as far as Reed was concerned; there was rarely much on Penny's mind—no complicated thoughts to cloud her conscience; no thorny dilemmas to keep her awake at night—but on this occasion, she surprised Reed with a question. "Why do bad things happen to good people?"

This got his attention; it was a subject that interested him. "I wish I knew."

She waited for more. "I mean, do you ever wonder if our sick patients are being punished?"

Keeping in mind Penny's core beliefs, Reed considered the directions his answer might take them. He recalled a time in history when sickness was deemed to be cast down by divine intervention. "No, I don't think our patients are being punished by a higher power, if that's what you mean. I suppose it's possible that some people sleep poorly or get run down if they feel guilty or upset."

"Guilty about what?"

"About something they did. Something they regret. People punish themselves all the time." Reed settled back in his chair and tried to estimate where this was going. He glanced at Penny's belly and marveled at the life growing inside of her—nearly three months and hardly showing.

"I think all guilty people are eventually punished," she declared.

"Is that so?"

"Yes. I mean, sooner or later we must answer for our sins."

Reed tried to decipher exactly what Penny meant by *our sins*. Was she referring to him? Until then, her simple observations were easy enough to dismiss, lost in the glow of her innocence perhaps, and the possibilities captured his imagination. It was a detour he had assiduously avoided, the prospect of getting closer to Penny. Then just as quickly, the moment passed. The planets returned to their proper order, and Reed stumbled back onto safer ground, where proper judgment prevails and desire does not stray beyond idle contemplation. He considered the mistakes that ordinary people make every day, the lonely hearts that mix and match into odd pairs, hoping to find love, ignoring the truth that for every good fit there are a thousand bad ones. A relationship with Penny would be transient at best, followed by immediate regret and incalculable loss. "I take it you're not talking about sick people anymore."

She looked at him oddly. "I was thinking about Kathryn."

That got his attention. Reed had no desire to insert Kathryn into a conversation about sin and punishment. Still, he had to know where this was going. "Are you wondering why something bad happened to Kathryn?"

"No, I'm asking if you think she was punished." The tiny gold crucifix at Penny's collar twinkled. And it began to make sense. To a believer like Penny, Kathryn's secular views were unsavory. There had already been whispers at the Church of God about the timing of her death and its greater meaning.

"I want you to listen to me carefully," Reed said, "Kathryn was not *punished* for her beliefs or *lack* of them. Her death was the result of a random act of violence. Maybe she was killed by someone who felt a need to punish her, but I'm certain that she did nothing to deserve it."

Penny had no verbal objection. It seemed she'd gotten the answer she was looking for. She returned to the front of the office and left Reed feeling unsettled, a contrast of emotions tugging at him.

10

At the age of twelve, Kathryn was given permission, for the first time, to walk alone after school to work at her parents' convenience store. Weekdays at 4:00pm she set her books aside to sweep the floors, restock the candy and chewing gum, straighten up the magazine aisle and wheel crates of bottled water to the coolers up front. The customers generally approved of the well-mannered seventh grader, particularly the elders, who were more inclined to chat. *What a pretty girl you are. Shouldn't you be playing outside on a nice day like this? Don't you have homework to do?*

But the neighborhood kids weren't as kind—they looked at Kathryn oddly, as if she didn't belong. Still, she enjoyed helping her parents at the corner store, where she learned new phrases like *I don't give a rat's ass* and *Get the fuck out of here!* She found adult behavior amusing and predictable: there was Mrs. O'Brien, who always had a kind word to say, and Mr. Clarke who grumbled whenever his lottery numbers failed. He smelled like a cigar.

Kathryn's mother explained the rules of the cash register and showed her how to make correct change. Her father told her to make sure that nobody left the store without paying—and Kathryn obeyed without question, though it was generally her nature to be trusting. Only once did she see a vagrant slip a bag of potato chips into his coat pocket, and as he lowered his head and left the store, Kathryn did not say a word, not even to her parents. The next day she placed a dollar of her own money into the cash register.

One afternoon, a man in a leather jacket approached the front counter and cautiously looked around the store before turning to Kathryn. "You have Royales?"

"Yes sir, box of three or twelve?"

"Three."

"Anything else?"

"Yeah." He looked over Kathryn's shoulder and pointed. "I'll take that ten dollar scratch-off."

Kathryn made the transaction and shut the cash register drawer. She had a feeling the ticket would be a winner, a hunch that skeptics would quickly dismiss as coincidence and believers would embrace as a gift.

For dinner, she took a shrink-wrapped sandwich from the cooler and brought it to the storage room out back where she was allowed to finish her homework undisturbed. If time permitted, she returned to work for another hour or so until her mother brought her home. She ended each day reading in bed, waiting for her father to come home to say goodnight—or if she wasn't reading, she was usually writing something in her private journal or in a separate binder stuffed with unfinished stories in various stages of progress. Her battered dictionary was combed regularly for words, punctuated with dog-eared pages and yellow sticky notes. More often than not, she drifted off to sleep with the reading lamp on and assumed by morning that she'd been properly tucked in and kissed.

Truth be told, Kathryn was happy. She liked her life. The earliest trappings of her personality were apparent at the age of four when she placed a pinch of garden soil in her mouth and found the taste wasn't *dirty* as expected, but surprisingly clean and metallic. She found similar attributes in the simplest things. At the age of six, she collected a small group of insects—an earthworm, three ants and two spiders—and placed them with a few blades of grass in a plastic see-through cup to see if they'd get along. She perceived a certain harmony among them at first, unsure if they were merely tolerating each other as grown-ups often do.

Lying in bed that evening, Kathryn imagined her cup of insects forging a bond or a common language of sorts, but the following morning she found the earthworm dead and couldn't understand why. She didn't know at the time that the worm would have been better off alone. Instead, the two carnivorous species had targeted the larger worm for a meal and there was no place to hide. Kathryn learned an important lesson that day about interfering with the lives of others; she freed the remaining insects and never tried anything like it again.

Over the next few years, she accumulated a closetful of dolls given by relatives who had assumed that an imaginative child would enjoy them—but Kathryn had little interest in playing with dolls, so they remained untouched until one Saturday morning, when she emptied her closet and asked her mother to help her bring the unopened boxes to a local charity. It turned out to be a pivotal experience for young Kathryn, who discovered that she can bring joy to others with little sacrifice of her own. Years later, she would teach her own students that *a candle sacrifices nothing by lighting another.*

As they drove home empty-handed that day, Kathryn's mother could not hide a twinge of sadness for her daughter. It didn't make sense right away, but Kathryn soon recognized that she was not immune to being misunderstood, even by an adoring mother. For the rest of the ride home, she stared through the passenger window with a sense of calm that followed her into adulthood—warmth and affection for those who loved her, and a stronger connection to the greater good. The latter sensibility would sustain her during her shortened life, and millions would follow her example.

Her childhood bedroom was a shrine to the things she held dear: posters of wild horses and elephants, sketches of architecture from centuries past, a photo of the USA women's soccer team, and an eclectic mix of classic and contemporary books. Her parents noticed that she was spending more time alone than with friends her own age and wondered if she might be depressed or lonely, but there was no need to worry; Kathryn had a profound connection to all living things and never thought of herself as alone. It was a conundrum for the hard-working couple who wanted the best for their daughter but did not quite understand her. They had little doubt that Kathryn loved and respected them, yet they felt her drifting away.

Looking for answers, they joined the local Church of God, where they were assured that its Sunday Youth Group would satisfy the needs of a precocious child. It was their hope that the voices of others in prayer would draw Kathryn in and make her happy, and in the beginning it appeared to be true; her eyes were opened to the splendor of the church, its stained glass and angular spires, glowing portraits and icons, and the grand pipe organ that accompanied a choir of voices singing to the Almighty above. Kathryn felt the power of community and discovered early on that the congregation itself was the best part of the religious experience. What better way to elevate the spirit of a child than to place her on the shoulders of others?

In the years ahead, Kathryn worked diligently at her parents' store, where she learned more about the human condition. She befriended a homeless man who camped out in a nearby alley and regularly brought him food. The neighborhood had its share of trouble in those days, including isolated break-ins and acts of vandalism, yet Kathryn was unafraid; she could not imagine anyone intentionally causing harm to her or her family. But Kathryn's mother was not as confident; she noticed her young daughter getting unwanted stares from men and kept a watchful eye, as any good mother would. There was no question that Kathryn would someday become a beauty—it was just a matter of time—a prospect that frightened her mother for reasons she could not quite explain.

11

On the first day of tenth grade, the new homeroom teacher asked the students to stand one at a time to introduce themselves. When it was her turn, fifteen year old Kathryn James stood from her seat in the first row and said *Kathryn*—and Reed Palmer lost all bearing. The name *Kathryn* echoed in his thoughts, in her voice, until he emerged from his fugue to a sea of faces staring at him, waiting to hear his name. He rose to his feet and mistakenly said, "Kathryn."

By the time Reed managed to shout his correct name, it was too late, the classroom had already spiraled out of control with laughter. A frenzy of adolescent hoots and hollers was followed by a primal escalation of foot stomping and fists banging on tables until the teacher finally seized control. She gave Reed a sympathetic look and moved on to the next student as quickly as possible. He could not bear to see if Kathryn was laughing too.

In the semesters that followed, Reed and Kathryn were in different classes, a separation that fostered a restless longing. They shared an occasional smile in the hallway, but little more. Reed yearned for a chance to show her that he wasn't such a fool after all, an opportunity that seemed to take forever. Helpless to resist the urges that coursed through him, he cursed himself for wanting her so badly. That Kathryn had similar feelings for another might not have surprised Reed, though he would never have assumed or imagined to be the source of hers.

In the winter of their sophomore year, Reed was determined to make his feelings known. Vulnerable to rejection and mindful of the despair that would follow if his instincts were wrong, he purchased a Valentine's Day card, signed his name Reed and slipped it through an open slot in Kathryn's locker. For the rest of the day, he experienced the kind of hopeful trepidation only a teenager can; he looked up at the wall clock and down at his watch every few minutes, wondering how long it would take for an answer. Would she read the card and feel the same way? Would she save him from a lifetime of loneliness?

His answer came the following morning when Kathryn shut her locker door and passed him in the hallway without a word. Reed was tempted to ask for an explanation but chose instead to be a good sport and accept his fate. Had the card not been intercepted by an unscrupulous classmate, things might have turned out differently. Instead, Reed kept his distance and didn't bother Kathryn with his absurd romantic notions. Their subsequent encounters were awkward and ill-timed, their mutual misconceptions left unresolved, and life went on for both of them. A small circle of girlfriends and a reliable stream of books kept Kathryn occupied while Reed watched from the shadows with longing curiosity, the kind of humble deference reserved for celebrities more easily admired than approached.

*   *   *

The summer after high school graduation, Reed took a job as a lifeguard at a pool club across town. Tranquilized by the heat and the reflection of the main pool, he found solace from his perch high above, where he spent long afternoons thinking about college and a future without Kathryn. Children splashed at the shallow end, teens stood on line at the diving board, and adults swam at the center. On the patio behind Reed, large umbrellas shaded bald men with cigars playing gin and poker. A bead of sweat trickled down Reed's forehead to the bridge of his nose, and life was good enough as far as he was concerned; nothing really mattered atop the lifeguard's chair except the clamor below and the future ahead. By late August, the perfunctory work at the pool club had all but run its course.

On the Friday afternoon before Labor Day, Reed clocked out and headed to the bus stop with no particular plans in mind other than getting out of the summer heat to an air conditioned house. He found several people waiting in line, all wearing the same tired expressions. At once, a cluster of dark clouds rolled in and an errant raindrop fell. Moments later, a drenching deluge began to fall and nearly everyone ran to the storefronts for cover—all except Reed, who reached into his backpack for a folding umbrella. From his point of view, the downpour was a sight to behold. Torrents of fat raindrops pounded the scorching hot streets and sizzled into the air. Giant puddles swirled to the curb and were quickly spit out by overflowing sewer drains. Through it all, there wasn't a hint of wind. It turned out to be a decent moment, the kind of summer storm that makes a rainbow at the end.

Without warning, a pattering of footsteps came from behind, and before Reed could turn around, Kathryn had joined him under the umbrella. Kathryn James, of all people! Soaking wet, she laughed as her body bounced against his. The surprise made him laugh too. How incredible, the shock of seeing her. They'd barely spoken during high school and there she was, just a few inches away. It was the opportunity Reed had always dreamed about, a spontaneous moment with Kathryn. Never before had he experienced her so closely, the powdery scent of her skin, the cookie smell of her breath, details he'd only vaguely imagined.

He knew their mutual arrival in a confined space could be the chance of a lifetime, or equally disastrous, and since the summer was almost over and they were likely to go their separate ways, he was determined to rise to the occasion. He used every ounce of composure to hold the umbrella steady between them. A flash of lightning lit up the sky, and Reed instinctively placed an arm around Kathryn. They braced for the imminent blast of thunder that rumbled through the streets, shared stories about teachers and acquaintances, and laughed as if they had been friends for years.

When the clouds parted and the sun came out, a magnificent rainbow emerged, and an empty B78 bus came to a stop directly in front of them. Reed followed Kathryn to a bench seat at the rear of the bus where they made easy conversation and became genuine friends, an experience beyond his greatest expectations—so perfect that he sometimes wondered if it really happened at all.

12

During her freshman year of college, Kathryn had a favorite pair of baggy overalls that hid her feminine curves from the overzealous boys. One of them, a prelaw student named Bence Jones, had made his intentions clear, but Kathryn wasn't the least bit interested; with little apology she offered only polite indifference, a mere roll of the eyes to keep him away.

Intent on pursuing her anyway, he signed on as a photographer for the college newspaper and took countless photos despite her objections. Among his favorites was a close-up of Kathryn's sandal dangling from an otherwise bare foot. Most of his candid shots captured her engaged in ordinary activities such as walking to class or reading in the library. He memorized her schedule back and forth, lurked by her dorm window, even wandered into her empty dorm room during class hours.

By spring semester, he had befriended Kathryn's bookish roommate in an effort to get near, but to no avail; whenever he appeared at their door with a snack or a bit of gossip, Kathryn promptly folded her books and left the room. One particularly warm afternoon in May, he arrived with a tempting offer: a pair of cold vanilla milk shakes. Her roommate gladly accepted hers and poked a straw into the plastic lid, but Kathryn left her milkshake untouched, as if somehow knowing that Bence had, just a few minutes earlier, in the boy's bathroom, ejaculated in hers.

Undeterred, Bence overheard that Kathryn had grown fond of a boy in her journalism class, a handsome philosophy student named D'Ante Boyd. The news piqued Bence's curiosity not only because of Kathryn's interest in him, but because he suspected that D'Ante was more of a misogynist than Kathryn realized. Fooled by none of it, Bence observed his adversary's mannerisms with sneaking admiration. Like birds of a feather that navigate via imperceptible signals, they were inexorably drawn together, and to Kathryn.

As final exams drew near, Bence found the break he was looking for. D'Ante was short of tuition money and faced the possibility of transferring to another school. At first, Bence savored the news— but instead of rejoicing, he made the unlikely decision to help. He went to the bank, withdrew half of his savings and placed the money in a plain envelope. He stayed up late rehearsing the dialogue that would follow, confident in the belief that no victory is sweeter than one snatched from the hands of another.

The next morning, he saw D'Ante in the back of the student cafeteria. He patted the thick envelope in his pocket and took a seat across the table. D'Ante held a cup of coffee in one hand and a soft-covered book in the other. At the far end of the table, a pair of grad students lifted their trays and walked off, leaving the two young men alone. Bence leaned forward. "There's a girl in your journalism class named Kathryn."

D'Ante lowered his book, barely enough to make eye contact. He sorted through the women's faces in his journalism class and offered a shrug.

Bence persisted. "What do you think of her?"

"She's okay."

"She certainly is. I bet she's good in bed."

D'Ante turned a page of his book. "Why don't you go find out?"

"I would, but she likes *you*." Bence reached into his pocket, produced the envelope and slid it across the table.

"What's this?" D'Ante looked inside the thick envelope and quickly closed it. "What do you want from me?"

"I want to video the two of you."

"No way…" D'Ante pushed the envelope back across the table and folded his arms, curious to hear more.

Bence looked around and spoke in a hushed voice. "Look, this is the easiest money you'll ever make—and it's yours for a quick half hour. A hidden camera in your room, it's easy."

"Forget it. I can get in trouble."

"No way, she won't see a thing." Bence's words came out in short puffs, the weight of his father's law practice in every syllable. "The video stays with me and nobody will ever know."

"What happens if she won't come up to my room?"

"Then you get nothing."

"What if she wants the lights off?"

"Then turn them on."

The questions were predictable but necessary; without a written contract this was the only chance to define their terms.

"And if she won't go all the way?"

"Use your charm; do the best you can. Give me a video with enough and you can keep the money."

D'Ante had to think about it. As the seconds ticked off, Bence was confident that Kathryn would finally be delivered on his terms, forever at his disposal.

* * *

The next day, Kathryn received an unexpected dinner invitation from the handsome philosophy student. She gladly accepted and found a spring dress for the occasion, a choice that generated friendly teasing from her roommate. She used a light hand with makeup that evening and decided to allow D'Ante a single kiss and nothing further.

They met at a quiet spot off campus and shared a bottle of wine with dinner. D'Ante poured with a free hand as their fingers made innocent contact across the table. He nodded convincingly at Kathryn's opinions. In turn, she found him to be easy company, certainly more of an ordinary guy than expected. He was neither intimidating nor conceited as her roommate had warned.

On their way back to the campus, D'Ante gave Kathryn the impression that he was bored. With a conspicuous glance at his watch, he mentioned that it was getting late and he had to get up early. Kathryn wondered if she'd done something wrong. They stopped in front of the dorms, where D'Ante took her hand and thanked her for a nice evening. He gave her an obligatory kiss. Then he kissed her again. The sweetness of red wine lingered in Kathryn's mouth, her judgment swept up in the moment, and with modest reluctance, she accepted his invitation upstairs.

The furnishings of the dorm were Spartan, the room adequately lit for video. D'Ante convinced Kathryn to join him on a futon, where he took her in his arms and gently kissed her lips. Kathryn was vaguely aware that her bra was being unfastened and briefly protested, but she enjoyed the kissing and didn't want it to stop. For a moment, D'Ante drew back to gaze into her eyes and explained that he'd never met anyone like her before. Before she could respond, he kissed her again and lowered a hand to the hem of her skirt. Kathryn nudged him away at first, then surrendered, unaware that a video-cam above the computer was aimed at the futon.

Kathryn James lost her virginity that night. In the weeks that followed, D'Ante Boyd barely acknowledged her in class or elsewhere. He ignored her phone calls and transferred to a different school over the summer.

Years later, Attorney Bence Jones stood by the curtains of the living room and watched as his wife drove off to the mall. The assistant DA, known in the community as an ardent fund-raiser for the church, was considered to be an attentive husband and reliable neighbor. Once the coast was clear, he retreated to a heavy bookcase, reached behind it for an unmarked DVD, and in a well-rehearsed motion, drew the curtains closed.

13

Penny stepped into the lounge to pour herself a cup. Reed smiled weakly and glanced toward the door to see if Shirley was nearby. The coffee maker exhaled. For the time being, it seemed they were alone. Before Penny could say a word, Shirley stepped into the lounge and took a cup from the cabinet, unaware that she had become the center of attention. With a clockwise twirl of the spoon, she looked curiously at the others and left the room unconcerned.

"I promise I won't get you in trouble," Penny said.

Reed was hardly reassured. He retraced the steps of their friendship and the clues he might have missed, the way she handed him a chart but didn't let go right away. He suggested that they get back to work. "We can talk about this later."

He waited outside the exam room, unsure if he had made a terrible mistake. On cue, the door opened and Penny emerged with a lighthearted grin. Reed cast aside the implication and directed his attention to the woman waiting inside, a young mother of two named Sally Fine. It was her second visit for the problems of headache and fatigue. Reed was concerned that she was hiding something. Her thin frame rattled inside an opalescent silk blouse, a light fabric buttoned high on the collar by a cameo pin. Her hands were tightly clasped over a yellow sweater folded neatly onto her lap. The bones of her knuckles pressed beneath the pale skin of her fingers.

Reed walked over to the sink and allowed a current of warm water to run over his hands. The soothing sound was a source of relief to both of them. Sally held tight to her sweater, anticipating the moment he would turn to face her. A pool of saliva gathered inside her mouth as he twisted the faucet knob and reached for a paper towel. "Okay, let's take a look," he said, turning to her while drying his hands. He placed a hand at the base of Sally's neck and gently probed. "Is this where it hurts?"

"Yes."

"What does it feel like?"

"Like my face is being pulled backwards."

"Any tingling of the fingers?"

"No, I don't think so."

He took the yellow sweater and folded it on a chair nearby. "Are you still having headaches?"

"Sometimes."

"What about the lower back, does that hurt?" He touched there.

She drew her knees together.

"You're a housewife, right?"

She nodded.

"How old are the kids?"

"Four and six."

He moved Sally's hair to one side, and she instinctively withdrew. Reed noticed something new, a bruise over her upper arm. The pattern was familiar: three elliptical marks suggesting the force of a grasp. "What happened here?"

"Where?" She folded her arms protectively; this revealed a second bruise.

Reed tried to think of a comforting word, something more fitting than his usual canned lectures about how to lift a heavy package or how to properly sit at a computer. He refused to dismiss Sally's physical pain as a metaphor for the emotional pain in her daily life; it would have been unfair to minimize her suffering that way. "Is everything okay at home?"

"Yes."

"I've seen bruises like that before," he said, inviting a more honest response. When he raised a hand to examine the back of her neck, she winced and withdrew.

"I'm sorry," she said.

Reed agonized for her. Poor self-esteem, an overbearing husband, and *she* apologized. It's always the same, the insomnia and exhaustion, then the pain. The ladies come in but the husbands never do. "I'd like to meet your husband. How about bringing him next time?"

Sally reached for her sweater. "Why do you want to meet him?"

"To ask him a few things," Reed said. "Maybe he knows where those bruises came from."

"I have to go," she said.

"Wait...."

Before Reed could say another word, Sally had already stepped off the exam table and headed for the door. Reed was tempted to block her exit but thought better of it. She would not want to be barricaded.

Penny stood by the doorway with a look of concern. "I'll set up the next patient." She nudged Reed toward his private office. "Go on, it'll take a few minutes."

"There must be a way of promoting human values without involving religion, based on common sense, experience, and recent scientific findings."

- The Dalai Lama

14

Monday night at the Ashford Arms was a good place to enjoy football on the big screen and hot open roast beef on rye (free with a two drink minimum). An illuminated mirror behind the bar drew attention to liquor bottles in all shapes and sizes. The thick aroma of mushroom gravy mixed well with inexpensive beer on tap—exactly what a neighborhood bar should smell like.

Reed walked in and took the empty barstool beside Father Francis, who'd already had his share. They shared a fraternal smile. "Margaret told me I might find you here."

"How is she?"

"Concerned. We're both concerned about you."

"You don't have to worry about me, my boy." He tapped Reed on the wrist.

The *boy* reference amused Reed who was only a few years younger. It seemed the father's collar created a veneer of experience beyond his years, a privilege Reed similarly enjoyed as a doctor. The bartender placed a coaster in front of Reed and stepped back. The father raised his empty glass and pointed to it but received no response from the bartender. "He's in a bad mood tonight," he whispered to Reed.

The bartender was not amused. He shook his head and backed away.

"Now, what were we talking about? You said the sister is upset about my driving."

"Actually, it's your drinking."

The father looked down. "Well I'm glad she's okay."

"She will be." Reed leaned in more closely. "I'm still not sure if we should be worried about you."

The father had to think about that. "I suppose I've had a few things on my mind lately." He used the tip of an index finger to rotate his round cardboard coaster until the words were turned upright; it was the name of a beer he did not recognize. He looked across the length of the bar and saw no ashtrays. The flat-screen television was new; the rest of the furnishings had been there for years, and a few of the patrons as well. "I don't know where to begin," he said. "Let's say there's a point in a man's life when everything makes perfect sense. And then sometimes the opposite happens."

"I'm not sure I follow."

A loud cheer spread throughout the room. Every few minutes a roar or collective gasp would direct everyone's attention to the flat screen. This time the father didn't notice; he looked squarely at Reed. "Tell me something, did you always want to be a doctor?"

"I guess so. When I was younger it seemed like a good idea."

"Yes, but did you feel a *calling* to the profession?"

Reed considered the source of the question; to a clergyman, a *calling* is more than an ordinary career decision. "I'd say it was a natural course of events. I was good in school and curious about the human body, so I became a doctor. I wouldn't call it a *spiritual* calling if that's what you mean."

The father nodded with approval. "Yes, that's exactly what I mean. Because a true calling is a rare thing; I've learned that there can be no *search* for a calling—a true calling must come to *you*."

"You mean a higher calling?"

"In my case, yes—I was called to serve." There was a hint of struggle in the father's voice. "And until now, I have served with all my heart."

"That's true for many doctors, too."

"Exactly my point," the father said.

Reed tried to understand. "Are you asking me this because you once thought about becoming a doctor?"

"A doctor, me?" The father laughed. "No, I couldn't tell a gall bladder from chopped liver. I was curious about your *decision* to be a doctor. Are you still happy with it?"

"I guess so. Are you happy with yours?"

"Sure, it's best job in the world."

"So what's the problem?"

The father grew quiet. He stared straight ahead at the mirror behind the liquor bottles. A blue vodka decanter glowed. "What would you say if I told you that I've been troubled lately by my role in the church?"

Reed was astounded. Coming from the mouth of a priest, the words were no less shocking than a doctor refuting basic anatomy.

The father received the response he had expected: silence and disbelief, indicative of the private burden he had been carrying. "Have you ever met my older brother?"

"No, Francis."

"Call me Frank, please. John became a priest five years before I did. After seminary, he was called to serve in Boston in a lively parish."

"So what happened?"

"Nothing serious—at least nothing scandalous, if that's what you're thinking. Quite the opposite, in fact; he's the toast of the town up there. If I had a drink right now, I'd propose a toast." Frank glanced at the bartender, who stood nearby with his arms crossed. "Anyway, we're all proud of him."

"Where is he now?"

"He's still in Boston, in line for a promotion. A priest can wait a lifetime for an opportunity like that. He's learned a great deal there, plus a few interesting things that might surprise you." The father paused. "Did you know that Kathryn and I were good friends?"

"Yes, I did."

"We were kindred spirits the two of us, so misplaced in this crazy world. We talked about everything, especially religion. I know she admired you a great deal."

Reed absorbed the sobering compliment and realized that the father's meanderings had yet to divulge anything remarkable. "You said you've questioned your role in the church?"

"I did?"

"Yes, was it something your brother said?"

"You mean John?" Frank's face brightened again. "You should have seen him play football in high school. When we were younger, I wanted to be just like him. Before I knew it, I followed him into the priesthood."

"Any regrets?"

"Regrets? No, it's been a good life."

Reed waited. "So, is there a God or not?"

"In the scripture there is. Did Kathryn ever tell you what she thought about God?"

"Yes, she believed that God is synonymous with love."

"That's right. Remarkable young woman, she didn't believe in the Holy Spirit yet she was the most spiritual person I've ever known. Her faith in humanity was as powerful as any I've ever come across. She believed that love is stronger than hate and that peace on earth is inevitable. I must admit, her ideas and writings have been transformative in my life. Her vision is one I've come to share."

Reed was gratified to hear the father's endorsement of Kathryn's ideas. "That's quite a departure for a clergyman. What about the gospel passed down for thousands of years? Have you become a heretic, Frank?"

"Not really." He searched for the right words. "I don't suppose you've ever had a personal crisis of some kind?"

"I've had my dark moments," Reed conceded, "but there was no personal crisis until Kathryn was killed. When she died I was traumatized more than I'd ever imagined. I couldn't eat or sleep for weeks. Would you call that a personal crisis?"

"Yes, I felt the same way when we lost our beloved Kathryn. But my struggle started a few months earlier, when I started to question my role in the church and my faith. Looking back, I might have been influenced by Kathryn in some way." The father admitted this without much difficulty, as if the words had been practiced during a private moment. "It's a terrible thing to doubt all you've been taught, all you've believed for so long. I can tell you firsthand that the burden of guilt was extraordinary, more than I could bear. So I talked to John about it."

"What did he tell you?"

Frank made a feeble attempt to get the bartender's attention. Reed gestured for him to go ahead and pour an inch. The bartender reluctantly unfolded his arms and did as he was asked. "John knew what I was going through," Frank said. "He knew about Kathryn's writings and felt the same way. He listened to my confession, not as a priest but as a brother, and the weight lifted from my shoulders. Of all the people to validate Kathryn's ideas, John arrived at the same conclusions. He said there are many others who feel the same way—more than you can imagine."

"Actually, I am aware."

"And there's more. Heaven help me, there's more."

Reed sensed a deeper struggle from the man beside him. He no longer saw Frank as a beleaguered priest but an ordinary man at the crossroads of his life, a thoughtful man whose lifelong beliefs were unraveling more quickly than he could handle. "What did John say to you?"

"Something remarkable." Frank set his empty glass aside. "A copy of Kathryn's manuscript has found its way to Boston, and another copy to Philadelphia. Her message is spreading faster than it can be suppressed. Mind you, there are scholars who are trying to suppress it, but it may be too late. There's already plenty of inertia there."

Reed tried to follow the father's tortuous path. "I'm not sure I get what you're saying."

"If it makes you feel better, it's been difficult for me too—but not for John. He's always been curious about issues of morality, the origins of religion, the path to enlightenment, and our ascension to wisdom."

Reed was fascinated; he'd always been similarly curious. "Your brother sounds like a thoughtful man."

"He's brilliant. Have you ever wondered about such things?"

"Yes, I have."

"You may be surprised to learn that there's an underground society that very few know about, a clerical think-tank where priests like John can talk freely."

"Is that so?" Reed was less surprised than he appeared. He'd always suspected a defiant band of progressives behind the scenes.

"It's true. John was taken into the embrace of others like him: men whose ascent in the church was rewarded with an opportunity to serve. For more than two hundred years they've met behind closed doors. The group has no name, just a shared ideology, and John fit in perfectly. He was drawn in by their dedication to address the problems of global hunger and literacy, issues that consumed his conscience for years, and not merely for existential kicks but to forge real solutions. As it turns out, according to John, their discussions have little to do with God or religion."

Reed nodded incredulously. A subculture of humanists among the old guard was remarkable. "But they still serve the church, don't they?"

"Of course they do. Remember, they've dedicated their lives to helping others; that hasn't changed. The reason they recite the scripture and receive confession is because it's what people expect from them—they want to feel better, and helping others feel better transcends everything else. Kathryn understood this. In fact, these men are living examples of her writings." The father had to smile at Reed's expression of disbelief. "Surely you must know that we're not just puppets up there. Do you really think the clergy accepts each written word of the Bible as sacrosanct? We serve our congregations because they need us. We set a good example and lead them from temptation. Someday it will be different, but right now *faith* is what people want."

"Not all people."

"That's fair. I'm aware that the church isn't for everyone, but if you listen carefully to Kathryn's message, then you know that being part of a congregation satisfies a basic human desire to belong. I happen to agree with her. And I think we should build on that idea. The concept that John and his friends like most about her manuscript is that they wouldn't have to alter the good work they'd already done. The fundamental ideals taught by Christ—kindness, tolerance, charity and brotherhood—resonate in every page."

"What about the Bible? Do you doubt the most celebrated book in history?"

"Not all of it. There's still plenty of good stuff in there."

"Let me get this straight: you're saying there's a group of clergymen who don't believe in the letter of the bible but go around preaching it anyway?"

"No, what I'm trying to tell you is far more important. In the short time since her death, our beloved Kathryn has struck a chord at the highest level. Her ideas have reached the hearts and minds of good people who've been waiting a long time for something like this."

Reed signaled to the bartender and asked for a pair of club sodas. "What about your brother. Where is he now?"

"Still in Boston; it's been a dream come true for a neighborhood boy. He's going to cherish those memories."

"So, what's the problem?"

"He's leaving. I spoke to him the other day and he's coming home. It'll be good to see him again." Frank's expression turned blank, as if his brother were coming home bodily intact but wounded in spirit. "Don't look at me like that. I don't want you to misinterpret what I'm saying."

"If I look surprised, it doesn't mean I disapprove," Reed said. "What's he going to do next?"

"He's planning something new, something incredible. His friends are raising large sums of money to help people in need, and they're doing it without any religious affiliation. They've gotten commitments from representatives of other countries, including leaders of every faith and an enormous financial pledge from the secular community as well—more money than you can believe."

"What about you, Frank? How do you feel about his decision?"

"I'm excited about it. John invited me to join the movement and I said yes. We're going to take off our collars and build something new from the ground up. There's a real need for this. We want to get started as soon as possible."

A touchdown on the big screen caused a big cheer. Reed motioned to the bartender.

"If you're willing," Frank said, "I'd like you to join us."

15

A week before her death, Kathryn walked to Lindower Park and found an empty bench. She liked to blend into the scenery and watch the children play. In her state of bliss, she noticed a dragonfly on the neighboring bench staring directly at her. She sensed that the dragonfly was sentient and shared an immediate connection. She said hello and watched it ripple in response. Its double wings gave the appearance of an antique biplane sitting on the tarmac. She perceived centuries of wisdom carried in its DNA from forebears that hovered over Cleopatra, Magellan and the Incas.

From fifty feet away, Howell tugged at his pants, lowered his head and approached. He flopped down beside Kathryn, close enough to touch his pants to hers. She accepted his company but shifted her body an inch away. In the weeks prior to her death, she'd become more distant and reserved. Mired in a strange and difficult time in her life, confused and distracted by mounting pressures at school, a veil of isolation had come over her. Wary of the vacant stares of men, their peculiar looks of longing and uninvited leering, she had stopped wearing makeup altogether and pulled her hair back into a less flattering style.

No matter, to Howell she was even more striking this way. He stared at the edge of her sleeveless shirt and inhaled stealthily as if capturing a trace. A familiar look of longing surfaced. He adjusted his glasses and raised his eyes to meet Kathryn's. "Did Reed tell you about the lecture?"

"Yes."

"What did he think?"

"He said it was good."

Howell suppressed a smile. "But you still don't approve?"

"I didn't say that."

Kathryn's disarming nature kept Howell off balance. He placed a hand over each knee to keep them still. "Think of the possibilities," he said, "healthy organs to replace the sick ones." He described the method of somatic cell nuclear transfer and the concepts he had proposed. If correct, it could bring new hope to millions.

Kathryn was only half listening. Overwhelmed by recent events at school and the mounting tide against her, she wondered why Howell had to be so provocative. "You're tampering with the beliefs of a lot of people," she said. "You can get into trouble."

"What kind of trouble?"

She stared at Howell curiously, as if trying to understand him better. He was at once a creative genius and unrepentant nihilist, a contradiction that underscored the constant struggle within him. He was inherently whimsical, yet he had difficulty accepting the spiritual needs of others. To say that Howell was atheist or agnostic would have been inaccurate—to be more precise, he was a *non-theist*. His unshakable *lack* of faith was an oddity to Kathryn, who accepted the rights of others to believe whatever they wished. But Howell was less forgiving in such matters; he censured any hint of faith or prayer. He felt the idea of worshiping the unknowable was absurd. Like so many scientists before him, he required proof of a divine presence, far more than scripture had to offer.

Ordinarily his opinions provided fertile ground for matching wits with Kathryn, but this time she wasn't in the mood. From several yards away, a woman pushing a baby stroller stopped in front of them and reached into a pouch at the side of the stroller to remove a pacifier. She placed it gently into the baby's mouth, uttered a few affectionate words, and moved on. Howell saw the look of approval in Kathryn's eyes. "Do you have any idea how many people are waiting for organ transplants?"

"Of course I do," she said. "That's why we need more donors." She turned to face him with renewed clarity. "I remember your brother. Is that what your research is all about?"

Howell brought a hand to the side of his shirt. Beneath it, a vertical scar ran down his flank, an empty space now. "It could save lives," he asserted.

Kathryn looked up at the trees. The rumblings of the park swirled around them, the children and their innocent laughter. With little more to say, Howell made a steadfast decision.

"The Lord kills and makes live; He brings down to the grave and He brings up again

- Samuel 2:6

16

The morning of Kathryn's death began like any other. A trace of pine soap filled the air of the old public library. Flickers of dust ascended to the light of the windows. Rows of honey oak shelves served as a backdrop for Kathryn, who sat cross-legged, deep in thought. The library was her favorite place in town. She loved its cavernous reading room where she could sit for hours amidst tranquil whispers muffled by whirling ventilator fans above. Green reading lamps centered on four rectangular tables were surrounded by a perimeter of aging books, a peaceful symmetry offset only by Kathryn's presence.

She held an open book in her lap, her thoughts far away. In her quest, she had spent many hours on line and in the library searching the archives for religious references to *love*, if not to understand it better, then to build upon what had already been accomplished—because to ignore the achievements of Michelangelo, Bach, Haydn and others, whose brilliant works were inspired by a higher faith, would have been intellectually dishonest. She believed the actual source of their inspiration transcended scripture, and she was determined to serve it up for modern consumption. Such were the ideas she put forth in her manuscript, *A Religion Called Love*.

At 11:45am, she gathered her belongings, stepped past the librarian at the front desk and pushed a shoulder against the heavy swinging door. A set of keys rattled in her palm. She lifted her face toward the sun and descended the wide steps to the sidewalk, where she breezed past a group of three young men, slightly bumping into one of them. With a polite *sorry-about-that* smile, she briefly looked over her shoulder and continued on her way.

Roused to mischief, the young men piled into an old white van and followed her. They slapped the vinyl seats beneath them and howled in unison to a pounding beat that shook the van. Unsure of where they were going or what they would do next, they watched Kathryn's taillights with growing anticipation—all except the youngest of the three, who was decidedly different. Caught in the current of the event with neither the strength nor means to change the course of their behavior, he howled with the others but hated himself for it.

Kathryn parked in front of her home, stepped across the driveway and climbed the steps of her porch. The white van circled around the block once more before slowing to a crawl. And the howling ceased.

PART 2

The investigation

17

Reed knew without question that a benevolent God would never have allowed such a thing. His mind racing, wishing beyond hope that he could have taken Kathryn's place right there, he rushed from her house to a neighboring block and jumped onto Howell's porch. He rang the doorbell twice then pounded on the front door until a light snapped on inside. "Hurry up!"

"Wait a minute!" Howell fumbled with the deadbolt and opened the door. Wearing boxer shorts and a T-shirt, he appeared to have just awakened.

Reed held out a plastic bag.

"What's this?" Howell took the bag and examined its contents: a cotton swab with a moistened tip. "Where did you get this?" He held it up to the sunlight.

Reed pushed his way inside. "Stop asking questions. I need your help. You have to take this sample and put it in broth right away."

"For what?"

"It's bad news..." Reed placed a heavy hand on Howell's shoulder.

"Jesus, what the hell is wrong with you?"

"Just get this in broth and I'll explain."

"If it's about my research, I had a talk with Kathryn about it..."

"For goodness sake, get these cells in broth! This *is* Kathryn!" He shoved Howell against the wall. "Do you understand what I'm telling you?" Reed took him by the arm and tried to steer him toward his basement lab.

Howell's glasses fell lopsided against the bridge of his nose. "Stop pushing me!" He looked down at the plastic bag. "Does Kathryn know about this?"

"You still don't get it? This is what's left of her! I was in her house a few minutes ago. Now come on, these cells might still be viable. We have to get moving..."

The color drained from Howell's face. He steadied himself against a chair and slumped down into it. "I can't. She wouldn't approve. We talked about it." He placed both hands over his hair and pressed down.

"Get up," Reed said, pulling at his arm. "This may be our only chance."

"Chance for what?"

"You know exactly what. You have to try."

"Forget it. Besides, it wouldn't be Kathryn, it would become someone else."

"But she might grow up to be just like her."

Howell shook his head. "Don't be ridiculous. Even if I can get a few of her cells to divide, then what? In a few weeks the cells will die without a host. We'd need a surrogate."

"Let me worry about that. I'll find somebody."

Howell stood up and straightened his glasses. He studied the contents of the plastic bag once more. "I'd have to prepare at least thirty nucleated samples from this sample."

"Now you're talking."

"With a little luck, maybe one good cluster will be viable for transfer."

"Come on." Reed led the way downstairs to Howell's basement lab. The ceiling was low and the air was cool and dry for his sensitive equipment. A blue florescent light buzzed over a pair of empty incubators. A minus-seventy degree freezer sat beside a dual headed microscope. Howell typed a password into his laptop then reached into a metal cabinet to remove a tray of gleaming instruments. He tore off its sterile wrap and placed it in front of the incubators. His movements were remarkably fluid and confident in these surroundings. For an instant, Howell stopped to give Reed a cautious look, a reminder that once they got started, their lives would never be the same.

The miracle is not to fly in the air or walk on the water, but to walk on the earth.

-Chinese Proverb

18

"You like undressing nuns."

"Not as much as you think," Reed said. "What I really like is undressing priests."

Sister Margaret smiled curiously. "Why is that?"

"I don't know, maybe so they can take off their collars and feel normal for a change."

"That's interesting," she said. "I get a kick out of seeing doctors pray in our church. It may surprise you that some of your colleagues actually seek guidance from a higher power."

"And many don't." Reed chose his next words carefully. "Sometimes I wonder if we'd be better off without religion."

Margaret drew back to get a better look at his face. "How can you say that? Do you have any idea what the world would be like without religion?"

"Well for starters you'd have to get a *real* job."

"You're such an ass!" She had to laugh. "Not everyone works for a paycheck. Millions of housewives work all day and barely get a simple *thank you*. You're lucky to get paid so well for what you do."

"You're right."

"And by the way, it may surprise you that some of your patients come to me before they come to you. Our jobs aren't as dissimilar as you think."

Reed had to admit a certain truth to that. "Maybe that's the problem; people confer too much faith in what you have to offer."

"You could say the same thing about doctors."

"I wouldn't argue with that. The prestige and credibility of the medical profession isn't always deserved. But really Margaret, what kind of prestige do you think the clergy should enjoy?"

"That's not for me to say. But if that's the way it is, you should learn to deal with it."

"I've had my share of practice," Reed said, patting the upholstery of the exam table. "People sit here all day and thank God when they recover from illness. They ask for my opinion about the power of prayer and what happens to the soul after we die, and for the life of me I can't imagine what I'm supposed to say. How can I possibly contribute to that kind of discussion?"

"You should be flattered that anyone wants to know your opinion. Most of us welcome the opportunity but are rarely asked."

"I know what you're saying Margaret, but I'm not the least bit flattered. Anyone can step up to the mike and give an opinion about religion. Who can really claim to know the unknowable?"

"If nobody can claim to know, then there must be a higher power after all."

"That's not what I meant." Reed was tempted to argue the point, but Margaret's glint of satisfaction got him to withdraw. After all, she was the patient and any means to help her feel better was fine as far as he was concerned. In that conciliatory moment, he found Margaret to be a kindred spirit, a woman whose calling to help others made perfect sense in the balance of things. In fact, she was more of a humanist than she knew, one who genuinely cared about people and elevated those around her.

"There's pain in your heart," she said out of the blue. "I can feel it from across the room."

"I'm fine," he said.

"No, you're not. You have a gift for touching others, but you don't allow yourself to be touched."

"I don't need to be touched."

"Yes, you do."

Reed couldn't tell where this was going.

She persisted, "Did I say something wrong?"

"No," he said. "But since you asked, let me ask you a question. Where do you think Kathryn James is right now?"

Margaret didn't hesitate. "She's in heaven."

They both smiled for different reasons. "It's incredible, the way you have no doubt about something like that."

"It's called faith," she said. "One day it will all make perfect sense to you."

Reed shook his head. "Not likely. Kathryn said *faith is what we allow ourselves to believe.*"

"She was right. It happens all the time, and it will happen to you. One day the Lord will appear in your dreams and His voice will guide you."

"Or maybe the opposite is true. You might wake up tomorrow and realize that it's all been a hoax."

Margaret took no offense. "Let me ask you a question. You loved Kathryn very much, right?"

"Yes."

"And she's gone now, but your love for her remains."

"So?"

"That's my point. Your love for Kathryn is undeniable, and even though she's gone from this world, your feelings for her are real as the clothing on your back. Why is that alright for you but you won't accept my belief in God? Why is my faith reduced to a delusion when your love for Kathryn is unquestioned?"

Reed had no immediate response. "You have me at a disadvantage, Sister. I didn't realize you're such a bully."

"You're the bully, telling others what to believe."

"I'm only trying to understand. It's true, my feelings for Kathryn are the same even though she's gone. Maybe that's what she was trying to express in her writings, that *love* is the lasting force inside us, not God."

"Or maybe it's God who *creates* the love inside of you. Have you ever thought about that?"

"Not really, I suppose it's a matter of perspective, or perhaps some of us are just more realistic than others. You may not want to hear this, but I've come to believe that the more intelligent a person is, the more secular he becomes."

Margaret was stunned. "That's the most arrogant thing I've ever heard."

"I'm just telling it like it is, like it or not. And I'm not the only one who thinks so."

"I'm well aware. I've heard the same thing from intellectuals, but it doesn't mean they're right. Having faith has little to do with intelligence."

"But it does. It's easier to convince a simple-minded person to have faith, especially if the reward is acceptance or forgiveness or eternal paradise, or if the consequence of disobedience is punishment. That's why you send children to Sunday school and teach them about heaven and hell, to get them when they're most vulnerable."

"I wouldn't argue with that." It seemed that Margaret was willing to find some common ground. "People need guidance at any age, not only from their loved ones, but from God as well. The church offers an anchor for their faith, a moral core for proper behavior."

"I respect your opinion," Reed said. "But if I were you, I wouldn't dismiss Kathryn's writings. Hers were not the musings of an ordinary woman. If you read her manuscript, you'll see there was plenty of meat on the bone."

"I have no desire to read anything that contradicts the Holy Scripture—you can't have both if one invalidates the other."

"I'm only suggesting that you should give her writings the attention they deserve before casting any final judgment."

"The only judgment that matters is waiting at the Pearly Gates. Besides, you of all people should know that I'm not the least bit obliged to give Kathryn's writings my attention. I cannot and will not stray from the only teachings that matter."

"I appreciate your passion Margaret, but you're missing the point. Kathryn had a lot to say about love and humanity. Have you ever read her manuscript?"

"No, but I've heard about it."

Reed smiled. "You might appreciate what she was trying to say."

"Give me an example."

"Alright, for starters, Kathryn posed the question, *what is it that good people all over the world have in common?* I'll give you a hint: the answer is not religion."

"Then what is it?"

"She said the answer is *love*."

Margaret shrugged. "What else?"

"She said the path to a meaningful life begins with accepting its impermanence. A simple, existential perspective brings joy to the moment."

"That's a rather Buddhist point of view," Margaret said, "and I'm not sure that it's true. Living with a sense of impermanence can just as easily bring despair."

Reed shook his head. "I wish Kathryn were here to explain it better. She'd tell you that it's alright to live and die without the promise of a hereafter. She might even tell you that she appreciated the time she had."

"As we all should. I wonder what she would consider to be a meaningful life."

"The answer is simple. I know for a fact that nothing impressed her more than the achievements of ordinary people—carpenters, teachers, waitresses, farmers, nurses—she admired all of them. She believed the potential for greatness hid quietly inside each of us, yet greatness is not required for a great life. She said a meaningful life requires neither script nor scripture, only a loving heart."

"I'm not sure that others will agree."

"Many already do," Reed said.

* * *

According to Kathryn, religion provided a sense of *belonging*. A secular stance, on the other hand, was more isolated and less festive by comparison. How to incorporate the benefits of *faith* into a secular state of mind was the challenge that beset Kathryn during her shortened life. If a sense of *belonging* fostered contentment among the faithful, then she was determined to find a common thread that would appeal to both religious and secular minds alike.

That universal element, she decided, is *love*. Powerful on its own, surviving like a reed in a hurricane, the human emotion of love had already endured the worst conflagrations in history and every example of mankind's unimaginable cruelty. Passed down through the ages, *love* was older than religion itself. To Kathryn, the seeds of modern religion, planted only a few thousand years earlier, had passed in the blink of the eye. She claimed that religion had been an essential stepping stone in mankind's social evolution, a source of tradition and rituals that kept families together and served as a foundation for moral good. She also believed the presence or absence of a supreme being was simply not for us to know. There was no right or wrong about it; she considered the musings of religious scholars as little more than the ruminations of an idle, imaginative lot. And since it was not her intention to impose her views on others, she kept her opinions to herself and wrote privately in her journal.

She recognized that religion was a great unifier, one that had opened countless doors to creative thinking, community work and charitable efforts that might not have otherwise achieved. She conceded that a belief in a higher power represented a crucial phase of mankind's development—it nourished humanity like mother's milk—and like infants that are inevitably weaned, there has been a natural tendency to move forward, just as there will be exciting journeys ahead, beyond man's current capabilities.

Her ideas attracted people of varying faiths, who found comfort in her stewardship of kindness and tolerance. With this in mind, she happily celebrated Christmas, the birthday of a timeless humanitarian, to share the spirit of the season for all the right reasons but the imaginary ones. She joined others with gifts and well wishes for friends and family to share the legacy of an exceptional man and proclaim collective good wishes for universal peace, a message that resonated in religious and secular homes alike. In fact, when Kathryn put forth the idea that *God is love,* she wasn't suggesting anything new; she was merely stating that the emotion of love exists without flesh or form. It's the spirit that flows between people of good conscience. It's the realization that love, like those who experience it, is imperfect. For this reason, Kathryn considered her own achievements and failures as equal foundations upon which to grow, and she expected nothing more or less from others. In this way, she was a true humanist.

19

The pastor's weekly sermons, typically rehearsed in front of empty seats, were lifeless and uninspiring. But he was confident that an adoring audience would soon resurrect this one. He put on his Sunday robes and stayed out of sight until the pews were nearly filled, then he emerged with an assertive smile and raised his palms for all to sit.

"My friends, I'd like to discuss something of vital importance this morning. It is written in Corinthians: *Don't you know that your bodies are members of Christ? Don't you know that your body is a temple of the Holy Spirit which is in you, which you have from God? Don't you know that the unrighteous will not inherit the kingdom of God? I tell you that neither the sexually immoral, nor idolaters, nor adulterers, nor male prostitutes, nor homosexuals will inherit the kingdom of God. Because every sin that man does is outside the body, and he who commits sexual immorality sins against his own body."*

"We thank the Lord for the blessings he brings us every day and for miracle of conception. It is through His blessings that we endure. Now imagine if the person directly at your side were stricken by an illness or accident—how tragic that would be—because each life is precious. But I'm sorry to say that we live in a society that allows God's precious gift of life to be cast aside every day, tossed into the garbage like dinner scraps. No, I am not talking about the sin of abortion. I am referring to something far more insidious and dangerous, the sin of stem cell research.

"My friends, stem cell research must stop now! Only God has the divine authority to create new life. And that life *must* be conceived between a married man and his wife. Anything else is sacrilege. Manipulating His creation is a sin, and we must see to it that it ends. For this reason, I want all of you to contact your elected officials and tell them that we've taken a stand. Stem cell research must stop now! We must refuse to stand by and ignore the desecration of God's work!"

Bence Jones sat in the front pew nodding enthusiastically for all to see. The pastor continued, "From the moment of conception, each of us is a unique creation of the Lord, conceived in His image. In this way, man is distinguished from the beasts—because only man possesses a soul. A scientist cannot create a soul. Only God can create a soul. Not only is the reckless manipulation of God's living tissue is sacrilege, but the technology doesn't work. Based on all of the available information, embryonic stem cells have created nothing but false hope for desperate people. The answers for spinal cord injuries, terminal cancer and Alzheimer's disease are not for us to know in this lifetime. The answers will come when the rapture delivers us to perfect health."

"It is written in Jeremiah, *'Before I formed you in the womb I knew you, and before you were born I consecrated you.'* And it is written in Psalm 139: *'For you formed my inward parts; you knitted me together in my mother's womb. I praise you, for I am fearfully and wonderfully made. Wonderful are your works; my soul knows it very well. My frame was not hidden from you, when I was being made in secret, intricately woven in the depths of the earth. Your eyes saw my unformed substance; in your book were written, every one of them, the days that were formed for me, when as yet there was none of them.'*

"The prophecy of the scripture speaks for itself. Stem cell research must be stopped. It is dangerously unsubstantiated and supported only by those who forsake the name of the Lord. We know that God works his miracles through doctors and nurses to relieve suffering, and it is only through Him that we get well. So I must ask you to contact your senators and congressmen and insist to them that stem cell research be stopped immediately! This blasphemous practice must never be used to raise the hopes of the sick! Let us pray together..."

Bence bowed his head. From the rear of the room, Robin observed with interest.

20

There's a difference between telling a lie and withholding the truth, a subtle difference that lies within the gray area of morality; one that became abundantly clear to the assistant DA while dining with a group of six men from the old neighborhood. They met on a monthly basis at the back of a family steakhouse to celebrate their dominance at the top of the food chain. Laughing and boasting like the boys they once were, the drinks loosened their tongues, and their unlikely tales of conquest were disrupted by one man's poorly timed confession about a fling he had enjoyed with Bence's former college girlfriend.

All eyes turned to the assistant DA and waited. That she was nothing special to Bence—they had only dated for a few weeks and uneventfully broke up—softened the blow, so he shrugged it off and gave his friend a congratulatory shove to let him off the hook. And the laughter began again. Then Bence's careless friend added the needless detail that their romp occurred *while* she and Bence were still dating, and the table fell silent once more. The men cautiously looked at one another.

Bence considered, in the instant that separates the weakest antelope from the rest of the herd, a few choice words to settle the score. To their surprise, he said nothing further. His response instead, muted by the sobering effect of the liquor, was an exonerating smile to show everyone that he was okay with it. In that instant, a young waiter dropped his large metal tray to the floor, a roar of cheers ascended to the rafters, and for the time being everything seemed alright again.

Bence finished his meal and was the first to bid farewell. Two weeks later, his careless friend was arrested on suspicion of solicitation. The evidence was weak and circumstantial, but serious enough to cost him his job and his marriage. A month later, his absence at the steakhouse was palpable. Bence insisted to his brooding tablemates that their friend's arrest was coincidental and nothing personal. It was the last time the group met.

* * *

"Have a seat, I'll be right in."

Detective Robin Noel stepped into the assistant DA's office and took a moment to look around. An airbrushed portrait of Bence and his wife seemed insufferably happy. Robin recalled her own family portrait of her half sober father and impassive mother with their best seasonal smiles alongside her two neanderthal brothers. She couldn't bear to think of Bence's family in contradistinction to her own. It was more damage than she wanted to fit in a single thought.

Bence walked in and noticed right away that Robin had a nice figure. No longer the skinny Tomboy from the neighborhood, she had filled out nicely. He remembered her as the younger sister of the legendary Noel brothers whose feats of artistry on the football field were the talk of the town. That Robin was an equally gifted athlete—she threw a baseball with pinpoint accuracy and wrestled her larger brothers into laughing submission—made little difference in those days. She was named captain of the church league softball team while her two brothers enjoyed full college scholarships.

Bence moved past her and took a seat at his desk. "What did you think of the pastor's sermon?"

"Interesting." Robin's abbreviated response was noted.

"Any progress with the investigation?"

"We're still putting the facts together."

"And?"

"A few leads, nothing specific..."

Bence put forth the same pretentious smile as in the airbrushed portrait. "Well, I'm sure you'll figure it out."

Robin didn't like his patronizing tone. "You were classmates with Kathryn in college, right?"

"We went to the same college but didn't see much of each other." He took a pencil from the desk blotter and rolled it in his fingers.

"How about Reed Palmer?"

"He went to a different college. I'm not sure where."

"What do you know about their friendship?"

"I wouldn't call it a friendship. I think he was really more of an acquaintance."

"Can you be more specific?"

Bence didn't have an answer right away. Robin wasn't sure if he was trying to remember or just stalling. "Maybe you should ask him."

"What about your relationship with Kathryn?"

Bence shifted upon hearing the word *relationship*. "We were friends, I suppose. We certainly had no reason to dislike each other."

"Would her college roommate agree with you?"

Bence held tight in his seat. "Yes, of course."

"What was her name?"

"I don't remember."

"But you're certain that she would agree?"

"Absolutely." He held on to Robin's stare and made an effort to keep still. If he had to staple his pants to the chair, he wouldn't allow himself to budge. He enjoyed matching wits with Robin. He found her intriguing, not only her choice of words and the tone of her delivery, but that she'd become so attractive. Her face was untouched by makeup or any attempt to beautify.

"Did you and Kathryn keep in touch after college?"

"We crossed paths a few times, but not much more."

"How about your wife; did she know the deceased?"

The term *deceased* got Bence's attention. *Deceased* as in murder investigation, a reminder that Kathryn James was dead and he was being questioned. The notion was at once unsettling and exhilarating. He caught a glimpse of himself in the mirror over Robin's shoulder. "No, I don't believe Brenda and Kathryn had never met."

"Would you mind if I talk to her?"

"You want to talk to my wife?" He did not wait for an answer. "It sounds like you're interrogating me."

Robin scribbled a note on her pad. "Not at all Counselor, I'm just trying to be thorough. One more thing; how well do you know Dr. Reed Palmer?"

"We knew each other a little in high school. I've also been to his office."

"For what?"

"I'm a patient of his." Bence knew that any personal information given a patient was confidential, and though he had no medical secrets to worry about, he enjoyed watching Robin's reaction.

She leaned in curiously. "How many times have you been to his office?"

"In the months since Kathryn's funeral, around three times." He raised a hand to his neck and rubbed it.

"Have the two of you discussed the murder?"

"Not really; it's been mostly small talk. But I should tell you, whenever I mention Kathryn's name he becomes quiet. I think it's a topic he'd rather not discuss."

"How do you know?"

"Just a hunch, like he's hiding something."

Robin nodded in agreement.

* * *

Driving in to the office, Reed felt a sense of disconnection from the rest of the world. In the lane next to him, a tiny red convertible contained a middle-aged man and his girlfriend, both windblown and chilled to the bone. Reed figured the sexy little car was more tempting in the warmth of the showroom. Off to the side of the road, a heavy woman in a banana yellow warm-up suit jogged uphill in utter agony. Sympathizing, it occurred to Reed that he was not the only one whose suffering was self-imposed. He pressed the gas and passed them all with a sense of detachment. Surely they couldn't feel the same anguish he did.

With a tap of the brakes and a turn of the wheel, he arrived at his office parking lot. Unsure of which part of his brain was responsible for getting him there, he gently touched the hood of the car like a trusted pet and stepped into the office, where life immediately made more sense. Shirley shook her head and pointed to her watch as he walked by. He fired up his laptop and checked the day's tasks. Then, after a pair of obligatory phone calls and a few scripts, he stepped into the treatment area and opened the exam room door. A familiar face caught him off-guard.

"I'm sorry. I know this is weird," she said.

Reed tried to think of something appropriate to say. Mallory Weiss after all these years; the timing of her appearance filled him with curiosity. She was a high school friend of Kathryn's, now sitting on his exam table. "What are you doing here?"

"I thought you might be able to help me." She brought a hand to the side of her neck.

"What's the matter?"

"I get a sharp pain behind my ear whenever I look up." Demonstrating it for him, she looked up and winced as if she had been poked by a pointy stick. Her complaint was brief and to the point. Reed sensed no hidden agenda, no other explanation for her visit.

"When did it start?"

"About a week ago."

"Did you hurt yourself?" Reed nearly blushed. He recalled Mallory's suicide attempt during high school. "I mean, did you slip or fall? Did you try to lift something heavy?"

"No." She looked down.

"Okay, let's figure this out." Reed circled behind to study the back of Mallory's neck. With a soft touch of the splenius capitis, the thin arc of muscle below her occiput, he slid a finger down its length and felt around for trigger points. The muscle should have been smooth as a banana skin. Reed took note of its texture and moved on to the sternocleidomastoid, from the mastoid behind her ear to the front of her neck. It felt tight and shortened. On a hunch, he placed a palm over the top of Mallory's head and pressed down with just enough force to close the trunk of a car.

"Ouch." She raised a hand to the tender spot behind her neck.

Reed suspected a disc or a spur pressing against a cervical nerve root. He asked if she felt any tingling in her hand.

"I'm not sure." She wiggled her fingertips.

The moment kept them in place, an opportunity to say something about Kathryn. But they allowed it to pass. Reed tested Mallory's antecubital reflexes, cranial nerves and proximal muscle strength. He screened for myofascial triggers, thoracic outlet, plexopathy and cervical cord pathology. He suspected an injury between C3 and C4, perhaps a pinched nerve. For a few seconds he looked into Mallory's eyes and felt a wave of nostalgia, a connection that evoked a better time in their lives when they were younger and everything was new. So many choices and all he wanted was Kathryn. At last, he asked, "Do you ever think about Kathryn?"

"Every day," she said. A veil of sadness fell over her. Reed sensed the depth of her grief, yet he doubted that she understood his. She stared blankly as if trying to read his thoughts.

"I think you have a pinched nerve," he said. "I doubt anything more serious than that. You'll be alright after a course of physical therapy." He could tell by her expression that she was skeptical. He wrote a set of instructions to his physical therapist and handed it to her. Then he typed a prescription into his tablet and sent it over the internet to her pharmacy. "I'm giving you something to relax your muscles. Take it an hour before you go to sleep for the next week or two and call me if anything gets worse." He was tempted to say more about Kathryn. "If you have any weakness or tingling in the fingers let me know and I'll set up an MRI scan."

"Thanks." Mallory stepped off the exam table and followed Reed into the corridor. Their walk to the exit was subdued, neither willing to admit anything further, and after a heartfelt hug and an unconvincing overture to meet again, she was gone.

* * *

Bence and Brenda Jones lived in a cookie-cutter home cluttered with colorful tchotchkes, childhood trophies, and movie posters. The familiarity of the old neighborhood served them well. They spent Sunday afternoons receiving friends after church, sometimes on folding chairs in the driveway, weather permitting. Brenda's Friday night spaghetti dinner raised enough money for a new set of bibles. Her last pancake breakfast helped purchase airline tickets for the pastor's annual retreat. Everything flowed fittingly in their provincial lives, an undisturbed predictability that eased the trauma of their home invasion. Bence arrived at 6:00pm hungry for dinner.

"Get out of here!" Brenda nodded in Bence's direction with a raised finger to suggest that she would be off the phone in a minute. He walked over to the stove and checked under the lid of a simmering pot. "Look, Bence is here. I'll call you back after dinner." She hung up and tip-toed in his direction to give him a peck on the cheek.

He allowed the kiss. "I have some news for you."

Brenda drew back to arm's length for a better look. "Don't tell me anything bad."

"It's nothing bad," he said. "It's just that... I think I know who killed Kathryn James."

Before Brenda could respond, a shout erupted from the home next door. *What do you think I'm made out of money? You buy those steaks like I'm made out of money! You spend every dime I make!* Brenda crinkled her nose and covered a guilty smile. When the yelling stopped, she noticed that Bence wasn't smiling. "You're kidding about Kathryn, right?"

"I know it doesn't make sense," he said, "It's just that..."

"Stop it! Just stop it for God's sake!" She covered her ears. "I can't believe you're still obsessing over that girl, isn't it enough that she's dead and buried?"

"No, it's not enough! I'm telling you that Reed Palmer was at her house that day."

"That's what you wanted to tell me?"

"Yes, that's it." Bence always had the last word. He left the kitchen to wash up, his mind giving little direction to the lumbering feet that pounded up the stairs.

Brenda glanced at her neighbor's window feeling less triumphant than before. She calmed the angry pot with a stir and set the table for a long, quiet dinner.

*   *   *

Stirred to insomnia, Bence knew exactly what he had to do. Brenda was awake at his side but had no desire to engage in another discussion about Kathryn. So she kept still. Until then, she was certain that Kathryn's death had put an end to her marital concerns. When morning came at last, Brenda went downstairs to make breakfast. Bence promptly closed the bedroom door and placed a phone call. After several rings, he heard the voice he was hoping for.

"Precinct, Detective Noel."

"Robin, I'm glad you're there. I have a question for you."

"What is it?"

"Are you aware that Dr. Reed Palmer was at Kathryn's house on the day of her murder?"

"Yes, I spoke to him about it."

"So, you're aware that just before she was killed, they weren't on the best of terms?"

"How do you know this?"

"Kathryn told me."

"She told you? When did this happen?"

"A few days before she died."

Robin doubted that Kathryn would have confided in Bence Jones that way. "I didn't know that."

Bence felt a brief sense of satisfaction. "Do you want to know more?"

"Yes, but I can't talk right now. I'll be in touch." She hung up and left Bence wondering if he had been taken seriously. She usually played her cards close to the vest and waited for her opponent to reveal something, but she felt that Bence had no intention of revealing more than necessary. Content to let the hand play itself out, she figured there would be enough time to question him on her own terms rather than on an unrecorded telephone call. She tapped a pen on the desk and thought about the assistant DA. His portrayal as a friend of Kathryn's held her attention. It occurred to her that she might have to look at the entire situation differently. She jotted down a note to herself and began to piece together the exact whereabouts of Bence Jones and Reed Palmer on the day that Kathryn was killed.

21

Robin pushed her way through the double doors of the Department of Forensic Medicine as if she had just walked into a saloon. She passed the information desk without asking for directions and got lost in a maze of corridors in which her nostrils were besieged by the pungent smell of phenol. She kept a loose hand over her nose and stepped into an unmarked room where two naked corpses were laying belly-up on rectangular steel tables. A bearded forensic intern in a surgical mask stood over one of the dead bodies and pulled a fistful of pills from its stomach. Robin checked the corpse's face: a pale 22 year old that smelled like beer and bitter sweat. At the next table, a masked woman lowered a scalpel into the belly of a homicide victim. A trickle of burgundy blood oozed onto the steel table and expanded into a dark sticky pool.

Robin did not mind the sight of blood, having seen her share of it, but when the blade sliced into the dead man's bowel, the powerful stench caught her off guard. She steadied herself long enough to exit through an open doorway to the corridor. Several yards down, she found a door labeled *Record Room* and stepped inside. A planter of thick green ferns hung from the windowsill. Soft jazz played from hidden speakers. A woman with cropped black hair and large earrings came forward. "May I help you?"

"I'm Detective Robin Noel." She produced her badge.

"Carmen Azar, records officer."

"I'd like to inspect the coroner's report of a homicide. The victim's name was Kathryn James."

Carmen was familiar with the crime. "That report hasn't been closed yet. All open cases are kept in the next room." She stepped past Robin to an adjoining door and returned with a CD and a written file. She removed the CD from its protective sleeve, loaded it into a desktop computer and stepped aside. "That should do it, just press *enter* and follow the instructions. Do you need anything else?"

"Yes, can you tell me who the coroner was?"

Carmen looked at the coversheet, where a single line had been left blank. "That's unusual. The coroner's name is probably recorded in a separate log up front. I'll be back in a minute."

Robin turned her attention to the computer screen. Unsure of what she was looking for, she randomly opened a file and scrolled through much of what had already been known to the public. There were dozens of interviews, local news clippings, background data on Kathryn's friends and family, employee information and crime scene photos.

One newspaper clipping featured a photo of Kathryn's face beneath the headline, *No Motive Found for Teacher's Murder.* Robin's memories arrived in succession. She advanced to a file labeled *coroner's report* and scrolled through, watching carefully for anything new or unusual. She painstakingly read the entire report depicting the murder scene: Kathryn's body position on the floor, the blunt trauma that occurred when her head struck the floor, the precise amount of dried blood at her hairline, an ecchymosed area at her left wrist suggesting the grasp of an attacker, the single broken fingernail beneath which a sample of the assailant's DNA had been obtained. Robin tried to imagine the crime itself. She hoped it was a quick death for her friend. Then she noticed something strange. "What the hell is this?" She called for Carmen. "This wasn't in the police report."

The cause of death was a fracture of the second cervical vertebra.

The coroner didn't speculate about the nature of the injury or how it might have been caused, only that it was there. Until then, Robin had assumed the same thing that everyone at the crime scene did, that the cause of Kathryn's death was blunt trauma to the head, evidenced by blood on the floor, a fractured skull, and a struggle with an apparent intruder. She finished reading the autopsy report and advanced to an assortment of photos taken at the scene and the morgue.

Carmen returned at last. "Detective, I found the information you're looking for. The coroner on call that day was Dr. Benjamin Bjork."

Robin turned off the computer. "I'd like to speak to him."

"I'm afraid you can't; he died several months ago."

"How did he die?"

"A heart attack they say. Actually this was one of the last autopsies he performed. I remember because we couldn't find a coroner to perform the autopsy on *him*. It would have been amusing if it weren't so tragic."

Robin wasn't amused. "I have one more question." She checked the margin of her notes. "What is a nulliparous cervix?"

Carmen knew the answer from personal experience. "It's the cervix of a woman who never had a baby."

"Thank you." Robin gathered her notes and found her way back through the maze of corridors to the harsh sunlight of the streets. Upon her return to the precinct she ignored the puerile comments that typically greeted her and found a ringing phone at her desk. "Precinct, Detective Noel."

"Robin, I forgot to mention something before. Do you remember a classmate from high school named Howell Martin?"

"Yes."

"Good, you might want to find out what he was doing that day."

Robin's greater temptation was to ask Bence Jones about his own whereabouts. "Thanks, I'll look into it." She jotted down the name *Howell Martin* and hung up without another word. Seconds later the phone rang again. She grabbed the receiver and shouted, "What?"

"Robin, is that you?"

She rubbed a tired shoulder. "Sorry, I thought it was someone else." She pressed a palm to her forehead and held it there. "No, I'm working late. Don't wait up for me. What happened to the doctor you were supposed to see? That's great." They shared a brief silence. "Let's make plans for Saturday, okay? Love you."

Robin was comforted by the news. Mallory was feeling better. She checked her list of names and resumed the search for Kathryn's killer.

22

Jacob Krauss was a retired cabbie who dispensed advice with brutal candor. His coffee-stained, powder-blue polyester pants and white patent-leather loafers always fit comfortably. His plethoric face and puffy eyes gave him an amphibious appearance. After forty years of driving his cab over city potholes, the mileage had taken a serious toll on his back. He rarely complained, though he enjoyed busting Reed's chops at every turn. "I don't see any diplomas on your wall."

Reed looked up at a framed poster of Magritte's *The Empire of Light* that featured a clustering of billowy clouds above a darkened landscape. Only Magritte knew if the day was about to begin or end. To Reed, it represented the promise of better times ahead—*always darkest before the dawn*. "Don't worry, I'm a real doctor."

"So how come no diplomas?"

"You're a real pain in the ass." He helped Jake get up onto the exam table. "There's probably a diploma hiding somewhere if you want to see it."

"Don't bother. My last doctor had a wall covered with them and he couldn't do a damn thing for me."

Reed looked around and saw no diplomas. "Actually, most of the things I do around here were figured out on my own."

"School of life, like me…" They shared a brief connection.

Reed took out his stethoscope and heard several wet crackles at the lung bases, a sign of early congestive heart failure. He detected the faint smell of cigar smoke on Jake's clothing and pictured him with a racing program in one hand and a hot dog in the other, but he was wrong. Actually, he knew very little about Jacob Krauss other than the stories about his cab. "You never mentioned anything about your family."

"There's not much to tell. When I was young like you I thought about getting married. But there was only one girl for me, just one girl and she wasn't interested."

Reed waited for more. "So what happened?"

"She wasn't interested. She married someone else."

"And you never got married?"

"I wasn't looking. I didn't want anyone else."

Reed was surprised by his own curiosity, even more so by Jake's unlikely romantic musings. "Do you ever think about her?"

"All the time."

Shirley's voice came through the door. "Dr. Palmer, your 4:30 patient called to say she can't get out of bed. She wants to know if you can visit her on your way home."

"Who is it?"

"Tiffany."

Reed looked at his watch. The day was progressing well. A brief stop after work wouldn't be a problem. "Tell her I can be there around six thirty." He noticed that Jake was grinning. "What's so funny?"

"Tiffany?"

"That's right."

He looked carefully at Reed. "I know it's none of my business, but this Tiffany wants you to come over to her house after work?"

"You make it sound like I should bring a chaperone."

"No, I'm saying you shouldn't go in the first place. This girl, how old is she?"

"Nineteen."

"Nineteen!" Jake coughed his back into a spasm. Before he could catch his breath he tried to speak again. "Nineteen and... and she can't get out of bed?"

"I'm glad you're so amused." Reed returned his stethoscope to Jake's back and heard the ominous crackles again. He wondered how much longer his heart and lungs would last. Without proper treatment his ankles would swell and he could drown in a sea of frothy pink sputum—or with the right care, he might survive another ten years.

"What's the matter, Doc?"

Reed rested a hand on Jake's shoulder. "We need to talk."

*   *   *

When the last of the patients had gone home, Shirley placed the phones on service and shut down her computer.

Reed came to her side. "How about taking a ride with me to Tiffany's?"

"Can't, I have to get home." She zipped up her coat. "Did you ask Penny?"

They glanced down the corridor where Penny was standing in front of a mirror, adjusting her bra. "It's okay, I'll be fine."

Penny passed between them. "See you guys tomorrow."

Shirley followed her through the door. Reed stayed behind for a few minutes to tidy up, shut all the lights and lock the front door. He stepped outside to the empty parking lot where darkness had fallen. A flood lamp swayed beside his car, the last in the lot. He opened the trunk of his car and removed a black doctor's bag, a relic bequeathed by a retired obstetrician; it contained an old stethoscope, a penlight, sterile gauze, swabs and tongue depressors. Hidden at the bottom of the bag was an emergency medical kit, suture material, syringes and needles.

He tossed the black doctor's bag onto the passenger seat and drove off. The streets were oddly silent that evening, as if an undisclosed curfew had been imposed. Reed imagined families huddled around kitchen tables discussing the day's events, all safe and sound. The image produced an existential tug in his mind, a source of private contemplation, or at least a welcome distraction until he turned onto Tiffany's block. He slowed to the curb and parked but didn't get out of the car right away. A distinct restlessness brewed inside of him. The more he thought about what he was about to do, the more he realized that Jake was right. He had no business visiting her.

From the driver's seat, he called Tiffany and advised her to see him in the office in the morning. And he took off. A series of synchronous lights brought him home to his driveway where he gathered his belongings and returned to the warmth of his house. He placed the black doctor's bag onto a credenza near the front door and dropped into his favorite leather armchair, where he assumed a Lincoln Memorial posture, his limbs slowly giving way to the gravity of the room. Ten minutes later, the tapping of footsteps on the porch and the doorbell brought him back to alertness.

He opened the door and found two people standing there: a slender woman with short dark hair and a man in his late thirties holding out a badge. He turned on the porch light and recognized Robin's face.

"Dr. Palmer, this is my partner Detective Anthony DiPalma. Would you mind if we come in?"

"Sure." Reed gestured for them to enter.

Robin loosened her jacket and settled in. "It's been a few months since we last spoke. Have you thought of anything new that you can share with me?"

"Such as?"

"Who would've wanted to hurt Kathryn?"

"I already answered that."

"And?"

"I can't think of anyone who would have wanted to hurt her."

"But somebody did." She looked at Reed carefully. DiPalma pointed to the black doctor's bag and Robin motioned for him to open it. "Tell me about Howell Martin," she said.

"He's a friend of mine. You already know that."

"Tell me about the research he was doing at the time of Kathryn's murder."

"He had an interest in molecular genetics. It's rather complicated; I'm not sure about the details. Why do you ask?"

"I told you already, we're gathering information. We can count on you to cooperate, right?"

"Yes, of course."

"Detective, look at this." DiPalma found the emergency medical kit at the bottom of the black bag. Robin showed no immediate interest. She stepped between the men to the kitchen and stopped in front of a set of carving knives. She pulled each knife out of its butcher block foundation, studied each one from handle to blade and returned them all in order of succession. She drifted over to the refrigerator, where a calendar marked with names and dates held her attention. Reed came to her side and leaned in to see what she was looking at. When her cell phone went off with a vibrating buzz, Reed backed off. DiPalma vanished to the next room to rummage about on his own. Reed was tempted to see what he was up to but didn't want to appear anxious. He kept his place at Robin's side and nodded politely as she held the cell phone to her ear.

"Fuck it, I'm not staying on hold forever." She terminated the call and called out to DiPalma, saying that they had to get back to the precinct. Before leaving, she asked Reed for permission to take the black bag to forensics. "I'll get it back to you as soon as possible."

"Keep it as long as you like," he said.

She scribbled a few words and handed it to him. "This is a receipt. I may have a few more questions so please keep yourself available."

"I'm not going anywhere." Reed stood like a sentry as Robin followed DiPalma outside.

23

"You'll never guess who is back," Penny said.

Reed peered into the waiting room, where Sally Fine was seated between two small children, all three keeping a wary eye on a large man sitting across the room.

"Should I bring them in together?"

"No," Reed said, "I want to speak to Sally alone."

Penny lifted a pair of lollipops and brought them out to the kids. Their response was muted but respectful. When their mother was escorted away, the older of the two got up and sat next to the younger one. Sally looked over her shoulder with a wave of unease, as if she had left them alone on a subway platform. She tried to reconcile the fact that their father was more likely than anyone in the world to endanger them. She was guided onto the exam table and informed that the doctor would be in shortly.

When Reed stepped into the exam room, he quickly noticed a new bruise on Sally's upper arm. He gave her an incredulous look. "Did you tell your husband about our discussion?"

"What was I supposed to say to him?"

"You were supposed to tell him to back off, to let him know that people are watching."

"That's why I brought him here, so *you* can tell him."

Reed folded his arms and measured the size of his own biceps. "I'll talk to him if you want me to, but the best thing you can do is gather your kids and get far away from him. Look at these marks…"

"How can I leave?"

"How can you stay? Do you really expect him to change?"

"People can change."

"If people can change then let's start with you. You must find the courage to leave, if not for yourself then for the kids."

Sally's maternal instincts kicked in. She knew the doctor was right. She would have to take a stance to protect herself and her children—but her courage was quickly doused by fear. "This was a bad idea; maybe I shouldn't have come." She stepped off the exam table and leaned toward the door.

This time, Reed placed a hand in front of her. "Wait, I have an idea."

"What are you going to do?"

"You'll see." He poked his head outside and motioned for Penny to join them.

"Don't make me say anything in front of him."

"You won't have to."

Penny came to the door. "Yes?"

"I'd like you to bring Mr. Fine in to join us. And do me a favor, check on the kids every few minutes to make sure they're okay."

Sally grew quiet and pale, especially when her husband was brought into the room. He was larger than Reed had expected, with the kind of menacing presence that raises one's primal defenses. Unshaven with a square jaw and a flattened crew cut, his sleeves were rolled up just enough to reveal a tattoo of an angry feline. He stood with both hands tucked into his pockets and shoulders slightly shrugged as if he had been called to the principal's office—the typical bully's demeanor in the presence of authority.

"Thanks for coming in." Reed matched the force of his grip. "I'll come right out and say it, Mr. Fine. I'm concerned about your wife. This constant bruising has me worried."

"Worried about what?" He glanced in Sally's direction.

She raised a hand over of the bruise marks.

"It could be a platelet problem, a vitamin deficiency—even leukemia can present this way. Sally and I had a discussion about it. Maybe it would be better if you and I spoke privately." Reed opened the door and held it open.

Mr. Fine checked his watch as if he had to be elsewhere. He reluctantly followed Reed down the corridor to his private office. Reed shut the door and pointed to an armchair, but Mr. Fine chose to stand in defiance. It was an interesting moment to be sure, during which Reed's stare was held a bit longer than Mr. Fine appreciated. Reed had no intention of fighting the larger man, though he choreographed the possibility.

A knock at the door kept them in place. "Telephone, Dr. Palmer."

It was Shirley's voice. "We're a little busy in here," Reed said, keeping his eyes fixed on Mr. Fine's.

"I'm sorry, but a Detective Robin Noel says she needs to talk to you."

Reed's imagination rushed in several directions.

"Should I tell her you're busy?"

"No, I'll take it."

Mr. Fine smirked. Reed shoved him out the door and waited for Shirley to transfer the phone call. The nagging premonitions that had haunted him and the demons that stabbed at his heels were finally catching up. The time had come to explain the unpleasant truth to Robin.

24

Robin Noel rang the doorbell of Kathryn's parents' home. She'd been there a few times during high school and once more since the funeral to speak with Kathryn's father. When the door opened, a familiar face appeared. "Mrs. James, I'm Detective Robin Noel, investigating your daughter's murder."

Kathryn's mother offered a welcoming smile; not the expression of a grieving parent but a well-mannered woman greeting an unexpected guest. She guided Robin to the living room. "Can I get you something?"

"No thanks." Robin looked past Mrs. James to a photo of Kathryn taken during high school. Unlike the yearbook photo disseminated to all the newspapers, the larger 8x10 color photo captured the details of Kathryn's hazel eyes. "Your daughter and I were friends."

The older woman didn't recognize Robin at all. She nodded with the polite understanding that Kathryn had many friends.

Robin sympathized without disclosing that this was not just another homicide case. When Robin accepted the challenge of finding Kathryn's killer, she put her personal life on hold and culled every dead end that would have fooled a lesser detective. She admitted no special interest in the case to anyone inside the precinct. Only one person knew how important it was to her.

Robin felt like she was standing on hallowed ground. Every trinket rekindled a memory of Kathryn: the photos, the diplomas, each a reminder of their unlikely friendship. They first met during a high school trip to the planetarium when they were seated beside each other in the dark. Looking up at the stars projected onto the ceiling, Kathryn listened attentively to the narrator, but Robin wasn't the least bit interested. It wasn't until the bus ride back to school that they actually spoke to one another. Kathryn shared her unpolished vision of the future, and Robin offered a more cynical view. Sitting behind them were two boys vying for their attention. The girls had little difficulty ignoring them and spent most of the bus ride discussing their respective interests: Robin had been considering a career in law enforcement. Kathryn said she wanted to become a kindergarten teacher. She said she could think of no better way to influence society than by teaching young children, before their minds become hard wired, while they're still learning to make sense of the world around them and trying to distinguish right from wrong. Kathryn wanted to be there, to help them navigate the maze, to show them how and when to yield to authority without sacrificing integrity, to teach them how to be responsible and respectful citizens, and how to forge an ethical conscience that would sustain them for the rest of their lives. One teacher, she said to Robin, can inspire the hearts and minds of twenty children each year for thirty years—that's six hundred minds! Few professions can offer that kind of impact on society.

Robin listened but was unimpressed. As far as she was concerned, a kindergarten teacher supervises finger-painting and reads storybooks, not much more. Her own kindergarten teacher, a nice lady with thick ankles and strong perfume, made no particular difference in her life. She had no idea that Kathryn would influence far more than six hundred lives. And Robin would have a profound impact on one.

"I have a few questions Mrs. James, if you don't mind."

"Of course Detective, ask whatever you like."

"Thank you. I'd like to know if you've developed any new suspicion about what happened to Kathryn. Can you think of anyone who might have been upset with her? Anything she said to you before her death?"

"I suppose so, but I doubt that any of it would be helpful."

Robin didn't want to prompt Kathryn's mother with a lead that could influence her answer. "You've thought about it?"

"Yes, I think it must have been an intruder, probably a stranger who didn't expect her to be home. To consider anything else would suggest that someone actually planned to hurt her."

"That's the problem," Robin agreed. "Your daughter wasn't the kind of person that a normal person would want to hurt." Robin suppressed her rage by pressing a fingernail into her own palm and refocused on the purpose of her visit. More importantly, she wanted Kathryn's mother to stay focused. "Isn't there anything else? A dispute with a neighbor? A suspicious handyman? Anything that springs to mind would be helpful."

Kathryn's mother recalled an incident from many years earlier. She was unaware at the time, but the homeless man who lifted the bag of chips from the convenience store when Kathryn was twelve years old was named Jack. He camped out in the alley next door. As it turned out, he and Kathryn eventually became friends. Always grateful for whatever Kathryn could spare, a few coins or half a sandwich, he returned the favor by sharing colorful stories about his life and a few tales woven from yarn too implausible to believe. Kathryn loved each of his stories and found an excuse to visit the alley whenever she could.

"Do you know what the word *quagmire* means?" Kathryn asked.

"It has two meanings," said Jack. "Literally, it's a marsh or a bog, but most people use the word to describe a dilemma."

"I like that word," Kathryn said. "I'm going to use it someday."

One afternoon, young Kathryn stayed after school to participate in a committee meeting, and in an uncharacteristic lapse of responsibility had failed to notify her parents. When an hour had passed and she hadn't arrived at the store, the police were notified and seized upon the homeless man. Torn between the accusation and his concern for the child's welfare, Jack was clumsily reticent. Before he could defend his whereabouts, he was thrown into a squad car, stammering unconvincingly to the precinct for questioning. Ninety minutes later, Kathryn arrived at the store in a haze of innocence to everyone's relief, and the matter quickly diffused. Her parents hugged her repeatedly and explained that she should never do anything like that again.

Meanwhile, in the alley nearby, the homeless man disappeared for good. Kathryn thought about him from time to time during adolescence and beyond, summoning his colorful stories to help fuel her writing. In her frustration, she knew there was no means to track him down since there was only his first name, *Jack,* and he had clearly moved on. Six months after Kathryn's death and shortly before his own, Jack came upon a book titled *A Religion Called Love.* It would be the last thing he would read and it held his attention all the way through. One particularly uplifting passage contained the word *quagmire*, which made him smile. In his state of infirmity, he did not make the connection that the book was written by the same little girl he once knew—but he thought about her anyway, as he often did. He recalled her gentle kindness during his most desperate time of need.

"I'm sorry," Kathryn's mother said. It was clear that she knew of no such dangerous person in her daughter's life.

Robin would have preferred to see a hint of anger or despair from the grieving parent. Instead, the woman sitting before her was much like Kathryn: calm and composed. "Are you aware of the difficulties your daughter was having at school?"

"Yes, Kathryn had mentioned that several parents were upset at her. But the children adored her; the teachers made a point of telling me."

"Can you give me their names?"

"No, I'm afraid not."

Robin decided that a more productive discussion would require a different tact. "Mrs. James, I'm going to mention three names and I want you to tell me what you think of each one, okay?"

"Yes."

"Reed Palmer, Bence Jones, and Howell Martin." Robin took note of her own decision to place the names in that order. In her experience, the first hunch was usually the right one.

"Well, first of all, I doubt that Reed Palmer had anything to do with Kathryn's death. He and my daughter were dear friends, perhaps more. You should have seen the way they looked at each other. I'm certain that you can scratch his name off your list."

Robin smiled at the thought. "What about Howell?"

"He was an odd duck, that one. He visited Kathryn's house on occasion, usually when Reed was there. I think the three of them spent quite a bit of time together."

"Tell me about your daughter's relationship with Howell."

"They were friendly enough, as far as I could tell. Please don't take this the wrong way, but I don't think she was entirely comfortable with him."

"Why do you say that?"

For the first time, Mrs. James appeared to be unsettled. "You must understand, I'm not accusing Howell of anything," she said. "It's just that I think he had a little crush on my daughter. It was probably innocent enough, but if you ever met him then you know he can be rather persistent. I remember he once tried to win me over with his academic credentials and fancy talk about his research, but to tell you the truth, I never really knew what he was talking about. I'm fairly sure that Kathryn considered him a friend, but not the way he wanted. If you want to know more, you'll have to ask him."

Robin had every intention of doing so. "What about Bence Jones?"

"Who?" Kathryn's mother stared curiously at Robin. "That name doesn't sound familiar."

"They went to high school together. He's an attorney now, an assistant district attorney. He said he knew your daughter very well."

Mrs. James shook her head. "I'm sorry, she never mentioned him to me."

25

Robin returned to the precinct and found a sealed envelope on her desk, the words *Forensic Lab* written in bold cursive. She pried it open and read the report confirming that the brand of sterile swab found inside the doctor bag matched a remnant of paper wrapping found at the murder scene. A handwritten note at the bottom of the report linked both items to the same medical supply company. Additional DNA testing of a smudge of blood on the discarded scrap would take another few weeks.

Robin felt a surge of tension tugging at the reins of her neck. She stretched her arms outward, unaware that DiPalma had been watching. When he had first heard the rumors about Robin's personal life, he chose not to believe any of them. No way, he thought, not a woman like that. Months later, when she finally confided the truth to him, he knew two things: Mallory was lucky to have her, and she was the best partner a detective could hope to have.

Without warning, she grabbed the forensics report and stepped in his direction. "Let's go," she said, patting him on the shoulder.

He pulled the hot coffee from his mouth. "Where to?"

"To arrest Dr. Reed Palmer."

*   *   *

Budd's leather jacket covered a lifetime of markings. From his gray, bushy beard to his belt buckle, each scar and tattoo had a story of its own. Six months earlier, his motorcycle struck broadside into a Lincoln and flipped over it. Budd was thrown ten feet into the air before landing flat on his back. The event made the six o'clock news. Lucky to be alive, he suffered a ruptured spleen, a broken collar bone, and a herniated cervical disk. He spent two weeks in the hospital, where he progressed from intensive care to the medical ward and finally to outpatient rehab, where he improved, though not completely. An incapacitating pain shot from his neck to his shoulder whenever he tried to lift his right arm. Any attempt to ride his motorcycle turned out to be grueling as rehab itself. After an assortment of analgesics and epidurals, he resigned himself to the prospects of surgery.

At the eleventh hour, he sought an opinion from Dr. Reed Palmer, who had seen this kind of injury before. Reed decided that the location and nature of Budd's symptoms would likely respond to craniosacral therapy, and he was right—not only did Budd respond more quickly than anyone had anticipated, his spirits lifted and his demeanor softened as well. Along the way, Shirley befriended the soft-spoken man and ritually poked her head into the treatment room to see how he was doing. Budd fell into the habit of sticking around afterwards to chat it up with Shirley.

With a complete recovery on the horizon, it seemed each visit might be his last. Reed backed away from the table. "How's that?"

"Good." Budd rubbed the back of his neck and rotated his head from side to side.

"Alright, then I'll see you next week." Reed began to walk away.

"Wait a second." Budd held him by the arm. "Do you need your house painted?"

"Not with that neck and shoulder of yours. The last thing I want you to do right now is paint my house."

"Not just me, I have friends with a lot of time on their hands."

Reed looked dubious. "I've seen a few of your friends..."

"They're nice people once you get to know them."

Reed recalled his first impression of Budd's entourage and had to agree. "Let me think about it," he said, opening the door. To his surprise, he stepped directly in the path of Detective Robin Noel. Her partner, Detective DiPalma, followed closely behind and pushed his way into the exam room.

Budd quickly stepped away and reached for something in his back pocket. Reed reached out to Budd with an open hand. "Relax, I don't think they're here for you."

"Dr. Reed Palmer, you're under arrest for the murder of Kathryn James. You have the right to remain silent. You have the right to an attorney." While DiPalma fastened a pair of handcuffs, Reed made brief eye contact with Budd, one of the toughest men in town. Penny stared in utter cataplexy as Reed was ushered past Shirley to the waiting room, where he stopped in front of his bewildered patients.

"This is obviously a mistake," Reed announced.

"Move it." DiPalma tried to shove him out of the office.

"I should be back soon, probably tomorrow, but if you can't wait until then, Shirley will give you Dr. D'Souza's phone number."

The patients rose from their seats and taunted the two detectives, admonishing them for their misguided arrest. DiPalma tightened his grip and pushed Reed out of the office. Curious onlookers watched from the sidewalk as Reed was tossed into the back seat of an unmarked car. Robin dropped into the passenger seat in front of him. "Those are very loyal patients," she said. "Do they know they're protecting a murderer?"

"Is that what you think I am?"

"Well?"

Reed said nothing further. As they drove off, a low sun flickered through the treetops. A bright, dizzying strobe-effect forced Reed to look away; there was no escaping it.

26

Reed spent the next five hours in an interrogation room where he was asked dozens of questions about his friendship with Kathryn and his personal life. He tried to be candid and cooperative, but it seemed the detectives were dissatisfied with each response. By 11:00pm he'd grown weary with nothing left to say. He was ushered to a secure holding chamber, where he curled up onto a cot and promptly fell asleep. An uncertain amount of time had elapsed when he was roused to consciousness. He opened his eyes and saw Robin Noel standing on the other side of the bars.

She didn't speak right away, as if waiting for him to say something first. They stared at each other for a solid twenty seconds before she spoke. "I know you killed Kathryn."

Reed shook his head. "She was my friend. You of all people should know that."

She raised an envelope in her right hand. "You may *think* she was your friend, but I can tell from reading this that you didn't know her at all."

Reed rose from the cot and took a step toward the bars. "I've never hurt anyone in my life."

"You can stop playing innocent with me." She passed the envelope through the bars and observed his reaction. He removed a single piece of paper from the envelope and recognized his own handwriting. "Where did you get this?"

"That's not important."

It was a note that Reed had written to Kathryn only days before her death. By the time he was halfway down the page, the words became difficult to read, the paper too heavy to hold. His arms dropped to his sides and the paper fell to the floor.

"Hey!" Robin reached through the bars. "Don't play that shit with me! I know what you're up to, you murdering fuck!" She pushed herself away. "Fucking psychopath, I'm on to you!" She stormed off and slammed the outer door. A rush of air blew the letter across the floor.

27

Making the best of a bad situation is a dubious skill, and Reed was quickly gaining experience in this area. After his semi-catatonic display, he was brought to a small conference room where he was told to sit down and wait. A video camera at the opposite end of a long table pointed in his direction. Beside him, large square mirror was conspicuous as a hole in the wall. Reed took a moment to smile at himself, unsure if he was being watched.

After an hour of waiting, a well-dressed man stepped inside and identified himself as Dr. Arnold Jarvis, a psychiatrist. Reed offered a polite handshake, but Dr. Jarvis made no effort to touch him or anything else in the room. His begrudging manner suggested that he'd been drawn away from more important things. After stating the purpose of his visit, a routine personality inventory to determine Reed's reliability in court, he began with a series of questions:

"*What is your name?*"

"Reed Palmer."

"*Do you know why you're here?*"

"Yes, I've been suspected of committing a crime."

"*Which crime?*"

"The murder of Kathryn James."

"*Have you been arrested before?*"

"No."

"Have you ever used illicit drugs?"

"Yes, a few times in college."

Jarvis cupped a hand over a yellow legal pad and wrote a note to himself. He proceeded with a standard cognitive assessment: *Name the last five US presidents. Subtract seven from one hundred and continue to subtract by seven until I say so. What would you do if you found a stamped, addressed envelope on the sidewalk?* And so on…

"Have you ever thought of hurting anyone?"

"I suppose so."

"Have you ever thought of killing someone?"

"Only in the abstract."

Jarvis wanted to ask Reed if he was actually guilty of killing Kathryn, but he was not permitted. The rules of the interview required that he adhere to the formulaic questions.

Robin watched closely from behind the glass. Bence stood next to her. Just prior to the interview, he had made another claim that he was a good friend of Kathryn's, an assertion that did not go unnoticed. Robin was fairly certain that Kathryn had never liked him.

"Dr. Palmer, tell me something about your character."

"Can you be more specific?"

"Alright, would you consider yourself an honest person?"

"Yes."

"Would you call yourself a selfish person?"

"That depends on your definition of selfish. If you mean do my actions only serve myself, then my answer is no. But if you define it in a more *objectivist* way, that I selfishly enjoy helping others, then maybe I'm selfish after all." Reed knew that Sister Margaret would have enjoyed this.

Jarvis made a brief notation in the margin and ruffled his papers. "Okay, next question, *would you consider yourself a religious person?*"

"No," Reed said without hesitation.

"Do you think of yourself as a happy person?"

"If you mean do I whistle a lot and tell funny jokes, then my answer is no. I've never been happy or carefree that way."

"So you're unhappy?"

"No, I'm just a normal person." Reed raised an eyebrow in a lighthearted attempt to engage Dr. Jarvis' sense of irony, but there was little response. *What a shame*, Reed thought, *a calling to the mental health profession wasted on a dense automaton, concrete as the curb.*

"I wonder what Jarvis thinks," Robin whispered from behind the glass.

"It's hard to know," Bence said with relaxed authority. "If he thinks Palmer is crazy, he won't have to stand trial."

"Dr. Palmer, you were arrested and had a near breakdown, but you still think of yourself as a normal person?"

"I assure you, I'm normal as you are."

Jarvis didn't like that. *"Tell me, how do you define normal?"*

"It's not my place to define it."

"Give it a try." Jarvis sat back in his chair.

For the first time, Reed sensed a departure from the scripted questions. "Alright, normal is whatever we decide it is. It's a relative term that means nothing without a frame of reference."

"*How do you mean?*"

"I mean there are appropriate norms for each time and place. In my life I've decided what is normal for me."

"That's interesting. If *you* decide what is *normal,* then I suppose you don't feel committed to a larger ideal, the law for example?"

"It depends on which law..."

"*How about smoking marijuana?*"

"I don't have a problem with that."

Jarvis scribbled another note. "*Do you smoke pot?*"

"No, but I think it should be legal for those who do."

Bence muttered to himself from the adjoining room. "Palmer is too calm. You can tell he's guilty."

Robin wasn't so sure. She crushed her empty Styrofoam cup and tossed it into an overflowing bin. "You should've seen him in the holding cell yesterday. He was out of his mind. Now he looks more normal than the shrink."

"And that shrink has an important decision to make," Bence said. "Maybe you can help him."

"You know I'm now allowed to do that."

"Go on, have lunch with him. Find out what he's going to decide. Make sure he gets it right."

"Gets *what* right?" Robin glared. "Is there something you're not telling me?"

"No." Bence looked straight ahead at the double mirror. "I only want justice for Kathryn, that's all."

28

Fixing a hearty breakfast for Bence was a task that Brenda Jones had come to accept. She knew that some wives did it for love, but she did it for herself. She found solace starting each day like a normal person, comforted by the aromas of toast and coffee. She squeezed fresh orange juice, cracked eggs and made oatmeal from scratch. She even timed everything just right so the butter on Bence's toast was soft by the time he took his first bite—and he basked in the illusion that Brenda did it all for him.

When he left the house for work each morning, Brenda got ready for the best part of the day, a quiet cup of coffee and a chance to listen to talk radio. She knew there was work to be done—the family room was cluttered and the breakfast dishes had piled up—they beckoned even as she consciously tried to ignore them. She finished her second cup and cleaned up the kitchen, then wandered to the family room and began to organize Bence's things into neat piles. She crouched beside the television and noticed a DVD jutting out of the player. Out of curiosity, she removed it and inspected both sides. It was unmarked.

Bence inexplicably jumped from his chair and darted out the office. When his secretary called after him, he did not slow down.

Brenda turned on the television and pressed the *play* button. She watched the video images unfold. The quality of the DVD was grainy and appeared to be homemade. It featured a young woman in

the act of being kissed and fondled. The sound was muffled and difficult to comprehend. For a minute the woman's face was obscured by
the shadow of a man's head until she emerged into better light and a
glimpse of the familiar face became clear.

Bence pounded on the steering wheel, his car interminably
stuck at a red light. He inched forward into the intersection, saw no
other cars coming, and pressed hard on the accelerator.

Brenda turned up the volume and squinted at the amateur
video. The details were blurred in the poor light. The young woman
featured in the forefront appeared to be oblivious to the filming, the
camera tucked away at an obscure angle. From the shadows, a voice
said "Open your mouth honey, we're just getting started." And her
heart sank.

Bence's car shot through the streets until he arrived at his own
block. He tapped the brakes, brought the car to a slow crawl and
parked in his usual spot. Once inside his house, he stepped into the
family room. "Honey it's just me. I forgot something." He couldn't
tell by the look on Brenda's face if she'd seen the DVD. He glanced
at the darkened television, feeling hopeful. "I left a few papers here
this morning." He scratched his chin and glanced around the room.
"Do me a favor and take a look upstairs, I think they might be on my
dresser. I'll keep looking down here."

Brenda obediently left the family room. Bence quickly dropped
to his knees to check the DVD player. He pressed the *eject* button
and heard a voice from behind.

"Is this what you're looking for?"

His heart skipped.

Brenda stood in the doorway holding a DVD.

Bence pushed himself off the carpet and turned to face her. "Did you watch it already?"

She nodded.

He reached forward and carefully took it. To his relief, she released it without protest. He would have preferred a more violent outburst, but Brenda wouldn't offer any. "It's not what you think," he said.

Brenda folded her arms and waited. She could think of no precedent for what he had done, no proper expletive.

Bence looked down and began to pace. "It all happened so fast," he said. "First there was a phone call with threats of blackmail. I thought about calling the police, then the video arrived and I didn't want to upset you. I'm so sorry you had to see it Brenda, I'm truly sorry..."

He tried to take a step closer but she put a hand up. "Don't come near me."

"What's wrong with you? How was I supposed to know they had a video camera that night? I couldn't see anything, remember? They hit me for God's sake!"

"None of those men had a video camera!" She began to weep. "You *knew* they were coming! I should have suspected it from the start. You never forget to put the alarm on. What kind of animal are you?"

"Brenda, I couldn't..."

"Get away from me!" She wanted to slap him in the face but could not bear the thought of touching him. The memories she had fought so hard to suppress were returning more clearly than ever. "Get out of this house. I never want to see you again."

Bence cautiously weighed his options, which boiled down to the end of his marriage versus the more damaging possibilities. Satisfied that he would have little difficulty explaining his wife's aberrant behavior to the rest of the congregation, he left the house with the unmarked DVD securely in his hands. He drove back to work at a leisurely pace, careful to obey the speed limit.

Upon his arrival at the office, he promptly locked the door, placed the DVD into his laptop and realized at once what Brenda had done. He had to smile, not so much at the images of their Cape Cod vacation, but out of admiration of her astonishing guile.

*   *   *

Dr. Arnold Jarvis slid his tray along the cafeteria line, seeking only the items that had been properly wrapped and dated. He moved sideways like a fiddler crab, stopping briefly to survey each option while keeping a healthy distance from others. After inspecting the bruise on a banana, he put it down and chose a plastic cup of yogurt and a sealed juice box. He counted his change in front of the cashier then carried his tray to an empty table at the far end of the cafeteria, far from the public element he assiduously avoided.

A tap on the shoulder startled him. "Doctor, do you mind if I join you?"

Jarvis looked up. "No, not at all…"

"Detective Robin Noel." She sat across the narrow table. "I'm curious to hear your opinion about the Palmer interview."

"You know I'm not allowed to discuss that."

"I mean generally speaking, do you think he's mentally fit to stand trial?"

Jarvis reached for a napkin to wipe his spoon. He poked a straw into his juice box and took sips in multiples of four. "I haven't finished my assessment yet."

"It's not that I'm worried," she said. "I'm sure you'll get it right." She leaned forward, her cleavage coming into view. "They say you're one of the most competent psychiatrists around."

Jarvis offered no humble qualification. He looked splendid in a crested blazer that looked out of place in a municipal cafeteria. A hint of silver at his temples gave him the credibility of an aging news anchor. He raked a hand through the back of his hair and sensed an instant chemistry between them, an intangible something. With a raised eyebrow, he opened the plastic yogurt container and twirled a spoon into it.

Robin watched in disbelief. "May I ask you a question?"

"Of course…"

"Do you think Dr. Palmer is competent to testify?"

Jarvis took another four sips from his juice box. "What do *you* think, Detective?"

"I think he's *definitely* competent to testify," she said.

"And I'm inclined to agree with you."

Robin was relieved to hear him say it, though she felt utter contempt. He could never understand what it was like for a woman to climb the ladder of an old boy network and endure the unrelenting backroom talk of other mediocre men like him. She leaned forward and allowed her breath to land on his face. "That's a lovely tie, Arnold." She pinched the fabric as if squeezing his balls. When he finally gulped, she let go and walked away.

29

Jacob Krauss ventured into the morning chill, his body half-covered by a terrycloth bathrobe that flapped in the breeze. He leaned over the curb to pick up the daily newspaper and threw a hand to his lower back. *Son of a bitch bastard!* His back muscles felt like Velcro ripping open.

He shuffled back to the house, cursing each gust of cold wind that shot between his legs. Once inside, he placed a pillow on a kitchen chair and lowered himself onto it. The first thing he noticed when he unfolded the newspaper was the headline *Doctor Questioned in Murder Investigation*. He adjusted his glasses and read about the troubled community doctor accused of committing a terrible crime, the most heinous in the town's placid history. A sidebar described the latest scourge of furloughs and mistrials that dangerously undermine an already broken judicial system. Another article offered a forensic psychiatrist's opinion about the complexities of a killer's motivation in general, while community leaders were given the chance to chime in about hardened criminals who were freed on technicalities that enabled them to kill and kill again.

Setting the paper aside, he reached for the phone and dialed.

"Hello?" The voice that answered was hoarse and half asleep.

"Finally, I was about to hang up."

"Jake, is that you? What the hell do you want?"

"To remind you there's a poker game this Friday."

"You woke me up to tell me that?"

"Yeah, and to remind you about the cash you owe me. Listen, as long as you're on the phone, I need a favor."

* * *

It was the faintest of sounds, three light taps of a bare knuckle on wood. Robin eyed her holster at the top of her dresser and left it there. She went to the front door unarmed and found Mallory Weiss standing outside with a grim expression. "What's wrong? I thought you were feeling better."

"I *am* feeling better. I'm feeling *a lot* better."

"So what is it?"

Mallory struggled to keep eye contact with Robin, always the more formidable of the two. "You know I've never interfered with your work," she said, stepping inside. "But I think you're making a mistake. Reed Palmer is the doctor who helped me."

"*He's* the one?"

"Yes, and he didn't kill Kathryn. I want you to leave him alone."

"Are you kidding me?" She stared Mallory into submission. "Have you forgotten what happened?"

"Of course I haven't, but what makes you think he's the one?"

"I have information."

"*Incorrect* information…"

Robin breathed steadily through her nostrils. She would have lashed out at anyone but Mallory. "You only want to help him because he helped you."

"That's right he helped me, and he never would have hurt Kathryn. I promise if you make him suffer any further, I will not forgive you."

Robin considered Mallory's request. Until then, they had agreed on just about everything. Neither was inclined to budge until Robin finally said, "I think you should go."

"Fine, I'll go." Mallory grabbed the doorknob and twisted it halfway. "But I'm telling you, you're wrong about him." She slammed the door on her way out.

"I'm *not* wrong!" Robin yelled through the closed door, pounding a fist against it. *Damn it!* She rambled back to a pile of loose papers and searched for a name that sprang to mind, one that had managed to slip through the cracks. She grabbed her badge and gun and drove to the edge of town, determined to prove she was correct.

Nearing the house in question, she slowed her car and checked the address in her hand once again. There was no movement on the streets, not even a group of children playing. The neighborhood had become unbearably quiet since Kathryn's murder. She rang the doorbell and waited.

The deadbolt un-clunked and a man with dark curly hair and glasses appeared. "Detective, I wasn't expecting to see you."

Robin responded with authority. "I need a few answers, if you don't mind."

"About what?"

"I think you know." She lowered her badge and stepped inside. She remembered Howell Martin from their discussion after the funeral and recalled his reputation as a gifted high school classmate—but as she surveyed his low-budget surroundings and his unkempt appearance, it seemed he didn't amount to much after all.

"Dr. Martin, I'm curious about your genetic research. What can you tell me about it?"

"What do you want to know?"

Robin checked her notes. "The somatic cell nuclear transfer experiments, did you keep any notes or records?"

Howell scratched the stubble on his chin and pretended to think about it. "I may have a few notes stored away."

"I'd like to see them. You wouldn't mind, would you?"

"If I can find them…" He stepped toward a door that led to the basement. "I think they might be downstairs." And he disappeared.

Robin let him go; she took the opportunity to look around. Since the beginning of her investigation, she believed that Howell was innocent. It was her gut instinct that he lacked the intangibles of a murderer, at least the menacing ones she had put away. Still, she was open-minded to any possibility.

Howell descended to the safety of his basement lab. He paced vigorously with lips tingling and hands trembling so badly that he had to open the tiny basement window to get some air. Fearful that Robin would become impatient and follow him downstairs, he grabbed a few notebooks and placed them in a box.

Robin waited at the top of the stairwell. When Howell returned, she grabbed the box and brought it to the living room to rummage through its contents. Howell watched with interest, still breathing heavily. "Are you looking for something in particular? I'm not in any trouble, am I?"

The tone of an innocent man, Robin thought. She removed a random notebook from the box and flipped through its pages unsure of what she was looking for, perhaps a key word or a sketch. "Dr.

Martin, in the course of your experiments, would there be any reason to use a sterile swab?"

"Yes." The academic question had a calming effect on him. "Only certain types of cells are suitable for somatic cell nuclear transfer. If necessary, I suppose some of them can be obtained with a sterile swab. For example, the cells inside a person's cheek, known as the buccal mucosa, contain abundant DNA."

"Have you documented this?"

"Yes, of course." Howell took the notebook and found a diagram of the method that can be used to obtain cells from the buccal mucosa. "Is this what you're looking for?"

Robin studied the diagram with mounting discomfort, not only because it tied Howell's experiment to the murder but because she was getting out of her territory. Science had never been her forte. "What were you trying to accomplish with these experiments?"

"To duplicate cells and harvest them, of course."

"For what purpose?"

"To replicate living tissue by placing a donor's DNA into a host egg."

"Did you?"

"Not exactly..." Howell felt his heart thumping under his shirt.

"What do you mean, *not exactly*?"

"I mean, it's still theoretical."

Robin observed. "Would you mind if I bring these notes to our forensics department? They might be important for evidence."

"Evidence for what?"

"There's reason to believe a similar swab was used at the time of Kathryn James' murder. Did you know anything about this?"

"Of course not." Howell maintained a look of surprise.

Robin allowed a few seconds to tick off. "You're friends with Reed Palmer, is that right?"

"Yes."

"Did he know about your research?"

"I think so…"

Robin took a step closer. For the first time, she started to feel unsure about Howell. "Dr. Martin, did you kill Kathryn James?"

"What? I mean no, of course not." He wanted her to leave in the worst way.

"She was a friend of yours, right?"

He nodded affirmatively, his mouth too dry to speak.

"How well did you know her?"

"I think…" He tried to swallow. "Maybe I should talk to a lawyer."

"A lawyer?" Robin moved closer. "*Now* you want to talk to a lawyer?"

Howell didn't respond.

Robin shook her head out of pity. "Alright, don't answer. Relax before you have a fucking heart attack." She ripped off a piece of paper and gave it to him. "This is a receipt for the notebooks. They'll be safely locked up."

"Go ahead…" he choked. "Go ahead and take them."

Robin carried the box outside. "And you can expect another visit from me, so keep yourself available."

Howell retreated to the door and locked the deadbolt. Once her car was safely out of sight, he stumbled over to the liquor cabinet and drank for a long while.

30

Reed tried to fall asleep, but it was no use; the light in the corridor was too bright and his mind was fully awake. A musty woolen blanket scratched against the skin of his neck and barely covered his feet at the other end. He actually started to feel sorry for himself, already ruminating about a life behind bars. The cracked paint and rusted pipes were early harbingers of the looming deprivation ahead. Unsure if a lengthy prison sentence would be a price too high for keeping quiet, he reconciled that in each lifetime a test of character is unavoidable. Primitive cultures test their youth with trials of resilience and courage—a walk over hot coals or a hunt with the elders—while modern society tests its inhabitants more randomly with a chance to hit rock bottom.

A tapping of footsteps got Reed's attention. It appeared that Robin had arrived with something new. "I thought you might want to have a look at this," she said.

Reed showed little interest.

"Don't worry, it's not another love letter." She put her hand out and invited him to take the single piece of paper.

Reed reluctantly took it and recognized Howell's handwriting right away, his wild trademark loops and a sketch of the tissue sampling technique. He couldn't help but smile at his friend's bizarre conception of thought—how anyone could make sense of the body's biologic chaos is extraordinary, and Howell did it with ease.

Robin didn't like Reed's look of approval. "You son of a bitch, you didn't tell him."

"Yes, I did." The sketch held his attention. "I told him the experiment failed."

"Like hell you did. We both know what happened." She waited for him to say more. "You're lucky to be behind those bars. If I could get my hands on you right now I'd wipe that smile off your face."

Reed knew there was no use arguing the point without confessing the entire truth. He handed the paper back to Robin. "Is there anything else?"

"Just one more thing," she said. "The trial will start in a few months, and I want you to know that I'll be in the courtroom front and center every day watching you wet your pants." She rested a hand onto the weight of her gun. "And when you're finally sent to jail, I will personally see to it that your cellmate is a three hundred pound psychopath who will use your asshole for his garage."

Reed had to laugh at the absurd image. "You know I'm being released on bond today."

"Then enjoy your freedom while you can, because when the jury delivers a guilty verdict I'll be the first one in the courtroom to celebrate. I might even throw a party."

* * *

Getting out of his cell was liberating as the last day of school. But with the trial nearing and vicious rumors spreading, Reed felt uneasy. Messages had accumulated on his answering machine with graphic threats that left little to the imagination. At the Church of God, Pastor Warren implored his parishioners to *leave the poor doctor alone*. He assured them that God alone will cast judgment—though he had also mentioned to the police that if someone felt the need to take matters into his own hands, there would be little he could do.

Reed could have stayed home and locked the door. He felt it would have been the prudent thing to do, yet he made the decision to return to his office, back to his devoted staff and patients. The moment he stepped outside to his car, a cracked windshield got his attention. He studied the zigzag design and drove to work unsure of what might be next. To his relief, a gathering of well-meaning smiles greeted him at the office. Shirley and Penny, ever watchful of his comfort, had booked a light schedule to keep him occupied but not overwhelmed. Feeling hopeful for the first time in months, he entered the exam room and said hello to his first patient, Mrs. Perlmutter.

Apparently, the hefty woman was annoyed that she had to wait. "I needed your help yesterday and you weren't available," she said. "You have no idea what it's like to be in pain."

"I'm sorry," Reed said, scrolling through her record. At the top of the page, Penny had recorded a complaint of *back pain* alongside a body weight of 230 pounds and a blood pressure of 182/96.

"Because my time is valuable too," she said. "I had to break an appointment to be here today."

Reed listened to Mrs. Perlmutter's laundry list of complaints. After a thoughtful inquiry about her diet and exercise habits, he performed a low back exam and decided that a low-carb, whole foods diet and a course of physical therapy would be appropriate. He prescribed a calcium channel blocker for her blood pressure, engaged her in a discussion about the importance of weight loss, and managed to get a smile out of her.

Later in the morning, Sally Fine stopped by with her children to announce that they would be staying with her mother for a while.

In full view of everyone, she thanked Reed with a kiss on the cheek, a gesture that became the source of lighthearted teasing for the rest of the morning. Then, shortly after lunch, an unscheduled patient named Richard Dupont insisted that Shirley squeeze him in. Reed agreed to see him despite the objections of his protective staff.

Mr. Dupont appeared to be healthy with a slender build, in his mid-thirties. He brought a complaint of weakness and tingling in his right arm and hand, symptoms that raised the possibility of neurovascular compression. During a thorough examination, Reed found his muscles entirely supple and free of tension. His deep tendon reflexes were brisk, his strength and sensation were normal and the exams for carpal tunnel syndrome and thoracic outlet were negative. "I'm sorry," Reed said. "I can't find anything wrong here."

"You must be missing the spot."

Out of curiosity, Reed performed the same provocative maneuvers. He didn't expect to find anything different, but he did find something unexpected. As if reading Braille, he had the distinct feeling that the patient was lying. "Your exam is fine. I can't find anything wrong."

Mr. Dupont showed no particular signs of relief. "By the way, I read about you in the newspaper."

Reed was struck by the comment. It seemed the problem was no longer the patient's but his. "What did they say about me?"

"They said you and the murder victim were friends." He waited for a response. "Terrible thing that happened to her..."

"Yes, we were friends." Reed moved behind Mr. Dupont and placed a hand to each side of his neck.

"Hey, take it easy." He tried to squirm away.

Reed tightened his grip. "You're asking a lot of questions. Are you a reporter?"

"Let me go." He tried to move but couldn't budge. "It wasn't my idea."

As if summoned, Penny opened the exam room door and poked her head in. Reed immediately relaxed his grip and withdrew. Penny noticed Mr. Dupont's reddened neck and put forth a look of disapproval.

Reed disappeared to his private office and began to pace like a caged tiger, as if trying to expel the indignity and the rage and whatever else was polluting his heart and soul. *What do they want from me?* He looked down and noticed a message left on his desk written in Shirley's hand. *Henry Johnson died this morning (sorry, I thought you should know).* He lifted the note and held it lightly between his fingers. He decided it's such an awful world, Henry was lucky to be rid of it.

"Dr. Palmer, are you okay in there?"

"Yeah, just give me a minute." He was tempted to pack it up and go home but decided instead to try once more. He returned to the front of the office where Penny and Shirley were standing by with looks of concern. Waving them off, he picked up his laptop once more and entered the exam room to see another patient, a forty year-old woman sitting beside a disabled boy who was nodding his head rhythmically.

"This is my son, Robert."

"Nice to meet you, Robert…" Reed kneeled onto one knee and extended a hand, but the boy didn't respond.

"He can't see you. He's blind." The woman turned and spoke in a firm voice. "Robert, give the doctor a handshake."

Robert extended a warm, floppy handshake and would not let go. He drew Reed in for a lengthy hug, and Reed's eyes filled with tears. His head bowed, his heart moved beyond reason, Reed wept for the little boy. He wondered how anyone afflicted with such a difficult start could carry on with joy in his heart. Robert's mother observed without judgment. She allowed Reed's catharsis to dissipate then placed a hand on his and said, "The bible says you're a loving person when your own pain does not blind you to the pain of others."

Reed nodded in agreement. The decorum of the exam room was restored, his issues placed in proper perspective, and he knew that Robert's mother had helped him more than he could ever help in return.

31

Anxious to get answers, Howell knocked on the door of Reed's home and prepared himself for a confrontation. The two had been estranged for months and had kept out of each other's way.

Reed opened the door, appearing less surprised than Howell had expected. No greeting was necessary.

Howell stepped inside. "Is there something you're not telling me?"

"What do you want to know?"

"I think you know what I'm talking about," Howell said. "As I recall, the incubation phase was going well. We had three viable zygotes that were ripe and ready for implantation. When you told me a hostess was unavailable, I shut down the experiment. That's how I remember it."

"Me too," Reed said.

"But there's one detail we haven't discussed."

Reed was bursting to say more, though his greater impulse was to protect his friend. "I don't know what you're talking about."

"Just listen to me for a minute. When I wrapped up the project and took a final inventory, I found only two zygotes. Do you know what happened to the third?"

"No, do you?"

"I was hoping you could tell me."

"I have no idea," Reed said. "Maybe the count was wrong."

"That's what I assumed, too. But that doesn't answer my other question: why did Robin Noel come to my house with questions about somatic cell nuclear transfer?"

"Who knows?"

"I think you do. That's why I came here, to find out from you what the hell is going on."

"I have a suspicion, but you're not going to like it."

"Try me."

"Alright," Reed said. "Why do you think Kathryn was so critical of your research? You said she was worried about the religious implications. She was already getting harassed at school from parents and teachers. I think that's why Robin came to see you, because she heard about the pastor who's trying to shut down your somatic cell research."

"Which pastor?"

"Pastor Warren, at the Church of God."

"But my work has nothing to do with religion," Howell said.

"You're right, of course." Reed was glad to change the subject. "I still wonder if Kathryn's beliefs were related in some way to her death."

Howell took a moment to consider the possibility. "I wouldn't be surprised."

"Think about it, she was a threat to a lot of people."

"Like who?"

"Believers," Reed said, "people who need magic in their lives and stories that are so unbelievable they *must* be true. They want to put their faith in a creator of miracles and sunsets and healthy babies..."

"That's rather cynical, don't you think?"

"Absolutely," Reed said. "That's the sad part. A thousand years from now, long after we've destroyed ourselves, archeologists from another world will find the dusty remains of titanium hips and silicone breasts and try to make sense of who we were, and I can assure you their conclusions will be no more accurate than our own. We haven't a clue as a species of what we're supposed to be. We use the terms *human condition* and *meaning of life* to add flavor to the journey, but in the long run I doubt that any of us is terribly significant.

"Speak for yourself."

"You know it's true. If we're lucky enough to survive, religion will be reflected upon as a curious phase of an imaginative people. Scholars will dissect its varied nuances and write dissertations about it. Museums will attract visitors to marvel at the customs of our forebears and share stories about the beliefs we once held dear, with a sense of relief that the human race didn't destroy itself."

"I'm not sure that everyone sees it that way..."

"That's perfectly fine," Reed said. "Kathryn took nothing away from them; she simply added a new voice to the discussion. She understood that people with different points of view still want to *belong*."

"That's where I take issue," Howell said. "People reject organized religion because they *don't* want to be defined by a group."

"That's what it boils down to," Reed said, "the contradiction of *belonging* by *not* belonging. Kathryn understood this paradox better than anyone, and in the end she was killed for it."

Howell considered the possibility. "Do you think that's what happened, that she was killed because of her beliefs?"

"Who knows? She's dead now so what's the difference?"

"Don't you think it matters?"

"If I said yes it matters, would that change anything? Any answer would be purely speculative; it's the kind of idle conjecture that fuels the religious debate. It's the gunk of human imagination that confers wisdom to random events: lightning strikes a tree and somebody is quick to point a finger at the charred remains. You wonder if Kathryn was murdered for any reason other than a random, violent impulse, and I'd like to know if there's a better reason."

"You have a bleak view of civilization," Howell said.

"I wouldn't argue with that. When Kathryn was alive, I was excited about the future. Now I'm not sure if I want to be part of it anymore."

"But you *are* a part of it. We're *all* part of it. It's not just a matter of perspective."

Reed looked at his old friend and empathized. Both suffered immeasurably in the wake of Kathryn's death—yet despite her absence, her voice was clear as ever.

32

The humanists sang loudly. They sang about love. They celebrated the lives of Jesus, Gandhi, Siddhartha (Buddha), Martin Luther King Jr., John Lennon, and others. They praised the virtues of real people like Muhammad who once said, "Do not consider any act of kindness insignificant; even meeting your brother with a cheerful face."

And their voices did not go unnoticed. Evangelical leaders considered the movement blasphemous. Muslims were outraged by the mortal references to Muhammad and demanded a jihad! Hasidic rabbis denounced Kathryn's followers as mere cult members and went further to dismiss the writings of a woman. The evening news feasted on the controversy. People on all sides of the argument chimed in to the voyeuristic delight of millions. The wide attention drawn to Kathryn's writings fueled a disturbing number of hate crimes. It made little sense that the musings of a young schoolteacher would become the epicenter of hostility, but there was no mistaking it. Dormant feuds that had been long settled were reignited with fresh points of view about the legitimacy of one faith versus another.

Kathryn's admirers tried to distance themselves from the debates, though every now and then an unsolicited quote from a well-meaning individual would surface and force the spotlight back in their faces. The humanists knew they needed a spokesperson to represent their interests, not a militant atheist with a paper trail but a newcomer with enough charm and wit to engage in thoughtful discussion—one who could persuade others to believe that it is okay to be loving and spiritual without being delusional. And they found one.

Kathryn had written in her manuscript, "If *love* is the ultimate human expression, let us share it with each other rather than waste it on the imaginary heavens." She explained that when a thousand Muslims kneel side by side on the carpet, it is not Allah that gives them strength, it is each other. Like the charge of a thousand batteries aligned, Christian worshipers inside a cathedral or Jews at the Wailing Wall are nurtured by the strength of community, a force that empowers each individual. And that force, she asserted, was love.

Kathryn would not survive to see it happen, but her ideas would expand more quickly than any religion in history. People who yearned for a secular yet spiritual experience spread the word and gathered at Sunday Assembly to share the joy. Humanist celebrants led vibrant services that promoted wishes for global peace and good health for all. New traditions were forged, lively songs were sung, teens were invited to join the adults, while younger children participated in supervised activities. Musicians, artists, athletes and others offered lessons free of charge. Classes taught by renowned professors and historians were available to those who wanted to learn about the real achievements of the human race and events that actually happened. On a local level, people found spiritual comfort in the stewardship of love for all living things, including the environment. They celebrated planet earth with a genuine sense of hope for the future.

PART 3

The Trial

33

Reed eventually hired a defense attorney named Schaeffer, a decent man and an adequate attorney, though his disheveled attire and conspicuous comb-over hardly embodied victory. It was out of shear benevolence or abject cynicism that Reed didn't bother to look for more suitable counsel. By contrast, the prosecutor was a woman named Belinda Carver, who was handpicked by the assistant DA to guarantee victory. She was known as *the closer*, with impeccable credentials and a stunning wardrobe. Formidable in any setting, Attorney Carver was accustomed to having her way inside the courtroom and elsewhere.

On the first day of the trial, Reed and Schaeffer agreed to share a cab to the courthouse to further acquaint themselves with a few details. The cabbie, a Muslim immigrant, eavesdropped on their discussion; he looked in the rear view mirror and recognized Reed's face from the local newspaper.

"What have you heard about Carver?"

"She's good." Schaeffer raised a loose fist over his mouth and stopped short of a yawn. "I've seen her in court a few times."

"Do you think she'll give me a hard time?"

"No question about it."

Reed didn't like the sound of that. "How do you think I should address her?"

"Address her? You mean address Carver?" Schaeffer was amused by the idea. "You won't get the chance. I'm not going to let you take the stand."

"But I want to tell my side of the story."

"Forget it, she will chew you up and spit you out, right in front of the judge and jury. I'm not going to let it happen."

"I don't understand. You're saying I'm supposed to sit on my hands and keep quiet?"

"That's right. Remember, a fish doesn't get caught if it keeps its mouth closed."

"What do you mean *caught*? You think I'm guilty?"

"What I think doesn't matter. The bottom line is they have a shitload of evidence that puts you right there in the victim's house. So I'm telling you, just be quiet and let them try to prove their case."

Reed left it at that. The trial hadn't even started and his lawyer was already waving the white flag. He only hoped that Schaeffer would be as persuasive on his behalf. Over the next few minutes, the tires of the cab hummed beneath them and Schaeffer closed his eyes. The cabbie broke the silence, "You are the doctor."

"Excuse me?"

"You are the doctor, the one in the newspaper."

Reed wasn't in the mood for conversation, certainly not this one. "Yes, I'm the doctor."

"You would be safer in my country. Where I come from it is permitted to punish a woman who defies a man."

Reed couldn't believe what he was hearing. "First of all, nobody defied me. Second, I didn't punish anyone."

The cabbie shrugged. "You are not Muslim."

"No."

"If you were Muslim you would understand there is only one judge. Praised be Allah, the only judge that matters."

"Not in an American court."

"Yes, it is written, 'Those who are with Allah are strong. He punishes the hypocrites and the unbelievers and He turns in mercy to the believers for He is oft-Forgiving.' Remember this when your day of judgment comes."

"You mean at the end of the trial?"

"No, at the end of your *life*. When my son was killed I knew he would spend the rest of eternity in paradise, because death is a blessing from Allah. But you are infidel who doesn't believe. That's why you're in trouble. It is written, 'To those who reject faith, Allah will not forgive them nor guide them to any path except the way to Hell, to dwell therein forever.'"

Reed had no response. For better or worse, the courthouse was only two blocks ahead. He jostled Schaeffer's arm. "Wake up, we're almost there."

Schaeffer opened his eyes.

The taxi stopped at the curb of the courthouse. Schaeffer paid the fare and Reed followed him up a dozen steps to a revolving door. They stopped at a metal detector, where they emptied their pockets and stepped through. A uniformed man passed a wand over their belts and shoes. Schaeffer said nothing as they refilled their pockets and guided Reed down a lengthy corridor to a small room where they sat and waited.

Schaeffer leaned back and took a moment to relax. Reed sat forward in his chair and wasn't the least bit relaxed. He found the room unsettling. He sensed the remnants of fear in that room, invisible particles ordinarily detected by wolves and other predators now present in sufficient quantity for a human awareness. An hour later, they were sequestered and brought into the grand courtroom—an interesting walk to be sure, during which the stares of a hundred pairs of eyes followed them to the defense table, the eyes of owls lurking in the stillness for lost mice. Reed recognized a few parishioners from the Church of God and smiled at one of them, a neighbor who quickly looked away.

Seated in the front row, as promised, was Detective Robin Noel. Reed offered a polite nod, to which she smiled in return—not a friendly smile but a gotcha smile. Turning back, Reed took a moment to admire the aesthetics of the courtroom. He saw no mercy in its design, no windows for daylight, and no inspirational peak reaching for the heavens. The judge's bench was made of hard cherry wood cut by honest, hardworking taxpayers: a jury of his peers.

"All rise."

At the front of the courtroom, an elderly man with wayward hair entered. Reed found himself standing with everyone, though he wasn't sure why. The judge adjusted his bifocals and climbed two steps to the bench, where a plaque engraved with the name *Burton Lambert* was displayed. Schaeffer and Carver approached the bench to receive the judge's instructions as the rumblings of the courtroom died down to a whisper. After a moment of implied negotiation, the two attorneys stepped back to their respective corners. Schaeffer entered a plea of *not guilty* and the trial began.

Carver stepped toward the jury box and stopped in front of a wooden railing. Dressed in a cream-colored business suit, her auburn hair was cut in layers and tapered in the back. She held a friendly gaze to one male juror, whose breathing noticeably deepened. "Good morning ladies and gentlemen. My name is Attorney Belinda Carver. I have been hired by you, the citizens of this state, to help convict this man, Dr. Reed Palmer, of the crime he committed, the murder of a young woman named Kathryn James."

She pointed a red fingernail at Reed's head. "I will show you evidence that puts Dr. Palmer at the victim's house on the day of her murder, and I will show you precisely why he had the *motivation* and the *means* to kill her." She glided a hand along the wooden railing. "Since there was no eye-witness to this crime, other than Dr. Palmer of course, the evidence you will be asked to consider is circumstantial. But it is powerful evidence you will see, evidence that will include the testimonies of several key witnesses."

Carver's voice was smooth and resonant. The jurors were entranced as children around a campfire. Reed sat back, convinced that her mission was less of an attempt to find the truth than to punish somebody for Kathryn's death. Her opening remarks were followed by a succession of testimonials from neighbors who were allowed to canonize Kathryn for the jury. Reed found himself agreeing with most of their kind remembrances, though he didn't see how any of it applied to his guilt or innocence. He had no choice but to keep his place.

Carver put the finishing touches on her opening remarks then sat down and slowly crossed her legs. Nearly every man in the courtroom glanced in her direction, and she knew it. His own attorney could have easily challenged her position but chose instead to lecture the jury about the law and their legal responsibility as jurors. His dry rhetoric would have been more appropriate for a probate hearing than an emotionally charged murder trial.

On the second day, Carver dug in her heels for a substantive fight. She produced a small piece of paper, roughly the size of a postage stamp, and submitted it to evidence. Explaining that it was a remnant of the wrapping used to contain a sterile swab found at the murder scene, she raised it to eye level inside a see-through plastic bag. A corner of the wrapping displayed in bold print the words that identified its contents. Carver explained its relevance to the trial and called her next witness to the stand, a forensic pathologist who approached the bailiff and got sworn in. He had a full beard and a tweed sport jacket. Reed noticed as he walked past that he smelled like pipe tobacco.

"Please state your name."

"Dr. Oscar Babinski."

Dr. Babinski's days as a hospital pathologist were largely behind him, though his credentials and eastern European accent were well suited for the role of expert witness. Carver stepped forward and asked him to state his profession.

"I'm a pathologist."

"Did you have the opportunity to review the autopsy of the murder victim Kathryn James?"

"Yes, I did."

"What was her cause of her death?"

"She died of a broken neck."

"Was it an accident?"

"No, there were signs of a struggle."

Carver handed Babinski the clear plastic bag. "Do you recognize the object labeled *exhibit number three*?"

"Yes, I do." He raised the item to the light and studied it briefly. "It's a remnant of paper wrapping. The writing on it states that the wrapping had once contained a sterile swab." Babinski returned the evidence to Attorney Carver. His manner implied continental breeding, the kind of patron that might send the wine back or insist on a proper fish knife for his sole. Schaeffer was not the least bit impressed.

"What is the purpose of a sterile swab?"

"There are many possibilities. In the medical field it is often used for wound dressings or to obtain a sterile culture."

"Please tell us if you think the swab might have belonged to the deceased."

"It's not likely, unless she was in the medical field."

"Are you aware that the paper wrapping was found at the murder scene?"

"Yes, I've been made aware."

Carver smiled. "You were also given an opportunity to review the items found in Dr. Palmer's medical bag, is that right?"

"Yes."

"Were the sterile swabs found in Dr. Palmer's possession the same as the one used at the time of the murder?"

"Yes, they were."

"How do you know?"

"Because this particular brand was only sold in bulk to medical professionals and it's been unavailable for years."

"Are you saying the sterile swabs in Dr. Palmer's possession would not have been seen in the hands of the general public?"

"Yes."

"Is it your opinion that a sterile swab was used at the time of Kathryn James' murder?"

"Yes."

"How do you know this?"

"A test was performed on a smudge of the sterile wrapping. There were fragments of DNA from a bloodstain and several skin cells detected by PCR."

"Blood, you say?"

"Yes."

"Please tell us, what is PCR?"

"The polymerase chain reaction is a laboratory technique that amplifies and duplicates protein molecules such as DNA. It is helpful in determining the origin of a tissue sample."

"Did you find an answer?"

"Yes." Dr. Babinski tightened his fists upon answering. Carver was the only one who noticed his subtle display of emotion.

"Please tell us doctor, to whom does the DNA belong?"

"The DNA detected was from the blood of Kathryn James and the skin of Dr. Palmer."

A muttering of voices echoed through the courtroom. "Thank you doctor. I have no further questions."

The judge glanced in the direction of the defense table. Schaeffer rose to his feet and moved toward the witness box. Before speaking, he raised a finger to scratch his head. "Dr. Babinski, you are an experienced pathologist, correct?"

"Yes, I have thirty years of experience."

"And you've served as an expert witness before?"

"Many times."

"Thank you. Please tell us, how accurate is DNA testing?"

"Nearly 100 percent accurate."

Schaeffer turned to Reed then back at Dr. Babinski. "You mentioned that a sterile swab was used at the time of Kathryn James' murder?"

"Yes."

"How do you know this?"

"As I told you before, the DNA from the swab…"

"Yes, the DNA, of course…" Schaeffer raised a hand to cut him off. "But you didn't answer my question. You said the DNA from the murder victim and that of my client were found on the remnant of paper wrapping, but how do you know the swab was used at the time of the murder?"

"Well, I can't be sure of the *exact* time…"

Schaeffer allowed Dr. Babinski's brief indecision to spread through the courtroom. "Do you think the sterile swab was responsible for the mortal wounds of the victim?"

Several chuckles were scattered about. Robin Noel turned to see who was laughing. Before turning back, she noticed a man in mechanic's overalls standing at the rear of the courtroom.

Dr. Babinski allowed himself to smile at Schaeffer's question. "No, Sir. The sterile swab was not the murder weapon. The cause of death was a broken neck."

"So it stands to reason that the person who broke Kathryn James' neck should be on trial. Tell me Doctor, do you believe the sterile swab was used prior to the murder, perhaps hours or even days before the murder?"

"No. The victim's blood on the paper wrapping would argue against it."

"So if the swab wasn't used *before* the murder, then when do you think it was used?" Schaeffer invited the witness to volunteer the only remaining possibility.

Dr. Babinski paused before answering. "I suppose the swab might have been used sometime *after* the murder."

"Thank you, Doctor. No further questions." Schaeffer stepped in front of Carver and returned to his seat.

Wasting no time, Carver invited her next witness to get sworn in by the bailiff. It was the psychiatrist, Dr. Arnold Jarvis. Immaculately dressed for the occasion, he wore a dark custom tailored suit—not quite black or charcoal but a shade lighter than freshly laid asphalt. His paisley tie was anchored by a stickpin, his hair neatly coiffed, his fingernails buffed and manicured. The corner of a monogramed handkerchief peeked out of his lapel pocket.

"State your name, please."

"Dr. Arnold Jarvis."

"Do you swear to tell the whole truth and nothing but the truth, so help you God?"

"Yes, I do."

Reed cringed at the rhetorical oath, as if Jarvis knew anything about Kathryn or the crime.

Carver began, "Dr. Jarvis, what is your occupation?"

"I'm a forensic psychiatrist."

"Did you have the opportunity to evaluate Dr. Palmer?"

"Yes, I did."

"What is your impression of him?"

Jarvis turned painstakingly to face the jury. "It is my opinion that Dr. Reed Palmer is dysthymic with a tendency toward bouts of hostility."

"Are you saying he's volatile?"

"Yes, volatile would be an accurate description," Jarvis agreed.

"Objection." Schaeffer stood at the defense table. "Leading the witness."

"Sustained."

Carver continued. "On what do you base your opinion, doctor?"

"My professional opinion is based on the specific character traits exhibited by Dr. Palmer, traits that are seen in those with a sociopathic personality disorder."

"Is it your opinion that Dr. Palmer has a personality disorder?"

"Yes."

"Please explain this to the jury."

"A personality disorder is a character flaw present at the core of antisocial behavior. It's the pathology that enables a person to kill without a guilty conscience, a common finding among criminals, especially murderers."

Carver seemed to approve. "Dr. Jarvis, most people would consider it insane to commit a murder. Do you believe the defendant is insane?"

"No, Dr. Palmer is quite sane," Jarvis said with a chuckle. "Insanity requires an organic defect, a medical diagnosis such as delirium or schizophrenia. I am certain that based on my very own assessment, Dr. Palmer is fully lucid. He makes informed decisions and he knows exactly what he's doing."

"So if Dr. Palmer committed the crime of murder, he did so knowingly, is that correct?"

"Objection!"

"Overruled Mr. Schaeffer, this is an expert's testimony."

Carver waited for Schaeffer to sit down. "Once again, Dr. Jarvis, in psychiatric terms, a mentally competent person such as Dr. Reed Palmer must be held responsible for his criminal behavior, correct?"

"That is correct."

"No further questions."

"Your witness, Mr. Schaeffer."

Schaeffer took an extra minute to review his notes before approaching the witness box. Dr. Jarvis was visibly irritated by this. He felt disdain for Schaeffer, the common lawyer, whose bad suit and obvious blue-collar roots diminished the legal profession. To be sure, Schaeffer was equally disdainful of Jarvis, whose snobbish manner and implied pedigree belied a mediocre mind. They smiled cordially at one another. "Dr. Jarvis, you used the term volatile to describe my client, Dr. Palmer. The word volatile is defined as lively, full of spirit…"

"No, I had intended to say he's dangerous and potentially violent." Jarvis quickly stopped, realizing that a question had not been asked.

Schaeffer smiled. "*Potentially* violent? Are you saying that Dr. Palmer is the *kind* of man who *might* commit a crime?"

"Yes."

Returning to the defense table, Schaeffer lifted a piece of paper and handed it to the judge. "Dr. Jarvis, are you familiar with the work of Monahan?"

"No, I am not."

"He wrote about the prediction of violent behavior in a paper that's been widely quoted." Schaeffer placed a copy of the article in front of him. "Would you please read the excerpt highlighted in yellow."

"I'm sorry but I did not bring my reading glasses."

"Then I shall read it for you." Schaeffer took the paper and found the excerpt. "It says, '*the best clinical research currently in existence indicates that psychiatrists are accurate in no more than one out of three predictions of violent behavior.*'" Schaeffer turned away from the witness box and faced the jury. "*Only one out of three*, Dr. Jarvis. And you're going to put a man's life at stake when there's a good chance that you're wrong about him?"

"I am not wrong."

"How can you be sure?"

"Because I am an expert in this area..."

"An expert, good. Then perhaps you can help us with something else." Schaeffer picked up a second manuscript and submitted it to evidence. "Your Honor, I'd like to quote from a paper written by

Halleck titled *Psychiatry and the Dilemmas of Crime*. Dr. Jarvis, are you familiar with it?"

"No, I am not."

"I see. To paraphrase, the article reads: '...*research in the area of dangerous behavior is practically non-existent. If a psychiatrist were asked to show proof of his predictive skills, objective data could not be offered*.'" Schaeffer handed the paper to the judge and stepped back. "In layman's terms, Dr. Jarvis, when it comes to patterns of dangerous behavior, it is difficult, if not impossible, to predict the actions of another. In fact, the best you can do as a psychiatrist is offer an opinion—and according to the literature, your opinion is likely to be *wrong*. Do you have any *evidence* that would implicate my client? Is there anything substantive you can offer other than your *opinion*?"

"No, Mr. Schaeffer, nothing other than my *expert* opinion… just as the jury will formulate *its* own opinion."

With a backhanded wave, Schaeffer turned his back on Jarvis. "No further questions."

Jarvis stood to vacate his seat, and Carver called her next witness. "Your Honor, the state calls Mr. Calvin Fine."

Reed showed no outward emotion, though he was impressed by Carver's resourcefulness. He would later learn that Calvin Fine, Bence Jones, and Attorney Carver were all members of the Church of God. Mr. Fine tried to appear docile as he climbed into the witness box. Wearing a long-sleeved shirt that covered his angry tattoo, he shrugged forward in the witness box and kept both hands tucked into his lap. He looked up at the judge with a deferential nod.

"State your name."

"Calvin Fine."

"How do you know the defendant?"

"He treated my ex-wife, Sally."

"What was wrong with her?"

"Nothing, as far as I could tell. I think the two of them had something going on."

"You mean an affair?"

"I couldn't prove it."

Schaeffer objected, and the judge gave Carver a stern look. "Please get to the point, Counselor."

Carver wandered toward the witness. "Mr. Fine, have you ever met Dr. Palmer?"

"Yes ma'am, when I brought Sally to his office."

"Did you speak to him?"

"Yes, he brought me into a separate room and locked the door."

"What did he say?"

"He accused me of hitting my wife."

"Were you hitting her?"

"No way, not even once. I love that woman."

"Then what happened?"

"He threatened me. He said he would hurt me if I didn't leave her. I thought about calling the police, but I knew she was already falling for him. What was I supposed to do?" Mr. Fine took hold of the bannister in front of him and looked down, as if he were about to weep.

Carver apologized for having put him through such a painful ordeal. "No further questions for this witness, Your Honor."

Schaeffer turned to Reed, who was impressed by Mr. Fine's performance. He anticipated that a showdown with Sally's husband would have to wait. Schaeffer declared that the defense had no questions.

Carver announced that her next witness would arrive in a few minutes. The judge allowed a brief recess, during which Reed considered the possibilities. Would Shirley be called to the stand? Would it be Howell? There was no choice but to wait. When the rear doors opened and the next witness appeared, Reed felt a jolt of rage. Penny was brought to the front of the courtroom looking unsettled, not so much by the spotlight but from the possibility of saying something harmful to Reed. Honest to a fault, Penny had no place in a courtroom; she lacked the predatory instincts required. Now in her third trimester, she glowed with an aura that caught the attention of several men, including the judge. One female juror in the front row was close enough to notice the absence of a wedding band and registered a look of contempt.

Carver took a moment to write a note in the margin of her legal pad then clicked her pen and took off her reading glasses. Looking up, she realized that Penny was prettier and several years younger. Carver drew a hand through her hair and glanced at the men in the jury to see where they were looking—and did not like what she saw. "Please state your name."

"Penny Brant."

"What is your relationship to the defendant?"

"I'm his medical assistant."

"Is that all?"

Penny wasn't exactly sure what Carver was referring to. "Yes."

"How long have you worked for him?"

"Three years."

"Is it fair to say that you know Dr. Palmer very well?"

"I guess so." Penny smiled at Reed and he nodded back.

"Please answer yes or no."

"Yes ma'am." Penny lost her smile.

Belinda Carver didn't like being called ma'am by a younger woman. She leaned against the juror's box and extended a long leg through the slit of her skirt. "Please tell the court, have you ever seen Dr. Palmer get angry or violent in the office?"

"Objection," Schaeffer raised a hand. "Circumstantial."

The judge agreed.

Carver turned to Penny once again. "Have you ever seen Dr. Palmer threaten or hurt anyone?"

Penny looked at Reed. "Not really."

"Not really?" Carver mocked Penny's voice. "We've just heard a sworn testimony from a patient's husband who felt that he was threatened with violence. Are you aware of any similar complaints?"

"No."

"Then let me help you. Do you remember a young journalist who was recently assaulted in the office? According to his deposition, Dr. Palmer nearly strangled him for no apparent reason, and when he tried to pull away, the doctor wouldn't let go. Please tell the court, did you know about this?"

"Yes."

"Were you concerned?"

"A little..."

"So you *were* concerned. Did you report it to anyone?"

"No."

"I see. Ms. Brant, I have one more question. It's a personal question but I must remind you that you are under oath. You're an unmarried woman who is carrying a pregnancy. Is Dr. Palmer the father?"

"Objection!" Schaeffer blurted out.

"Sustained." The judge wagged a crooked finger at Carver.

"I have no further questions."

Schaeffer turned to Reed with pleading eyes, anxious for a rebuttal. It was a golden opportunity for Penny to deify him in front of the judge, but Reed wanted no part of it. He shook his head protectively and placed a firm hand on Schaeffer's wrist to keep him in place. Reluctantly, Schaeffer withdrew. "No questions."

Judge Lambert scribbled a note and removed his bifocals. "Alright then, it's just about noon. Let's take a break until 1:30 PM." A crack of the gavel jolted everyone out of their seats and into the aisles.

34

Reed and Schaeffer were brought to a small room, where they were allowed to meet privately for lunch. They were each given a turkey sandwich and a can of iced tea. Schaeffer removed the cellophane wrap from his sandwich and began to eat right away. Reed observed with interest. Contemplating his fate, he was curious about the attorney sitting across the table. "You married?"

"Divorced."

"Got any hobbies?"

"Nope."

Ordinarily, Reed wouldn't have cared one way or the other, but as he considered Schaeffer's minimalist style, he wondered if he would end up paying a big price for it. "Mind if I ask you a question?"

"Go ahead."

"Why don't you let me tell my side of the story?"

"I told you, it's not a good idea."

Reed wanted to yank the sandwich out of Schaeffer's hands. "That's it? We've listened to two days of irrelevant testimony from people who hardly knew Kathryn. Doesn't that bother you?"

"Not at all. I told you to be patient and let them prove their case. Why is that so difficult?"

"Because this is my life! The jury thinks I'm some kind of menace, and you're doing nothing about it."

"You have a short memory. A few minutes ago I wanted to give your assistant Penny a chance to show everyone what a great guy you are, and you wouldn't let me. And what about your friend Sister Margaret? She would have been a terrific character witness and you refused to bring her in to testify."

Reed got up and shoved his chair the table. "You lawyers crack me up. You sit at ringside and cheer for a good fight but you're never in any real danger yourselves. Have you ever noticed that? I think you're all a bunch of cowards."

Schaeffer looked surprised. "Wait a minute, what do you have against lawyers?"

"It's not just lawyers, it's the whole damn courtroom, the artificial self-important absurdity of it. No matter what happens to me, you all get to go home at the end of the day."

"Now wait a minute…"

"Admit it, if you were accused of a crime, you'd *demand* to defend yourself. You'd take the stand in a heartbeat."

"Don't be so sure."

Reed sat down once more and stared at his sandwich. "You can't expect me to leave my fate in the hands of a jury that hasn't even heard my side of the story. I won't allow it."

"And I told you it would be a mistake. If you get up there to testify, Carver will get a chance to cross-examine, and I promise you, she will clean your clock."

"That doesn't sound very hopeful. You make it seem like I don't have a chance."

"I'm saying your best chance, maybe your *only* chance, is to keep quiet." Schaeffer began to eat again, though his chewing appeared to be labored. Reed watched until the silence wore him down. "Alright, alright…" Schaeffer said, flipping his sandwich back onto its paper plate. "This goes against my better judgment, but if you must testify, I won't stand in your way. Just do me a favor and try to look innocent up there."

Reed was amused. "*Look* innocent?"

"That's right, *look* innocent. It's all the jury really cares about."

* * *

A garrulous crowd returned to the courtroom, their belts tightened an extra notch. Schaeffer reviewed his notes and waited for the noise to settle down before starting. "Your Honor, the defense calls Dr. Reed Palmer."

Reed hesitated upon hearing his name—it was as much an out of body experience as he had ever known. All eyes were focused on him as he walked the interminable twelve feet to the witness box. With each step, the clicking of his shoes against the hardwood floor echoed like firecrackers in the gaping silence. He climbed into the witness box and waited for Schaeffer to begin with the questions they had rehearsed during the lunch break. Their plan was to offer the jury a cursory review of Reed's credentials, followed by a few softball questions about his community service and his friendship with Kathryn.

"Please state your name for the record."

"Reed Palmer."

Schaeffer hesitated before asking his first question. The look in his eyes changed perceptibly, as if he had something else in mind. "Dr. Palmer, did you kill Kathryn James?"

"No."

"Do you know who did?"

"No, I do not."

Schaeffer moved to the front of the witness box and maintained his position there. Reed tried his best to keep his attention focused on him, but it was difficult. Kathryn's mother had taken a seat in the front row, directly in his line of vision. He could only imagine what she'd been through and what she must have thought of him. "Dr. Palmer, can you tell us when you last saw Kathryn James?"

"Yes, on the day she died."

A few expletives rippled through the aisles. The judge's thumb moved in the direction of his gavel. Schaeffer remained focused. "On the day she died, Dr. Palmer?"

"Yes." Reed kept his hands clasped firmly together. He knew it was imperative to keep still and listen carefully.

"You were at Kathryn's home on the day of her murder, is that correct?"

"Yes."

"Why were you there?"

"I wanted to see her, to tell her something." A wave of reticence caught Reed off guard. He had never had to express his feelings like this before, certainly not in public.

"What did you want to say?"

"I wanted to let her know how I felt. It was important for me to say the words, *I love you.*"

Another torrent of angry voices erupted throughout the room. This time Judge Lambert lowered the gavel. "Settle down!"

"I only wanted to *tell* her, that's all!"

Schaeffer stood in place, unaffected by the commotion. "Go on," he said.

"I expected nothing in return. I only wanted to let her know."

"Are you saying that Kathryn was unaware of these feelings?"

Reed couldn't answer. The question didn't sit well with him, not only because it was a highly personal matter, but because he didn't know the answer. He reached for the pitcher of water and a cup.

"Dr. Palmer, I asked if Kathryn was aware of these feelings."

"No, I don't believe so."

Schaeffer acknowledged this with a nod. "What time did you arrive at her house?"

"I rang the doorbell at 11:00am."

"And how did Kathryn respond to your... um, to the admission of your feelings for her?"

"She didn't have to. She wasn't home. Nobody answered the doorbell. I'd forgotten that she usually went to the library on Saturday mornings. I stayed on the porch for a minute and left." An image of Kathryn's porch appeared in Reed's thoughts, the gray cement porch with the black wrought iron railings.

Schaeffer kept him focused. "Dr. Palmer, you returned to Kathryn's house later the same day, is that correct?"

"Yes."

"How much later?"

"About an hour later. I thought she might be home by then."

"Did you get a chance to speak to her?"

"No, I'm afraid not. I rang the doorbell, but there was no answer." Reed made fleeting eye contact with Kathryn's mother. "This time, the screen door was unlocked and the kitchen light was on. So I stepped inside."

"Was Kathryn there?"

"Yes, she was lying on the floor."

"Was she alive?"

"No. Her skin was pale and cold. I think her neck was broken." Reed scrutinized the sound of his own voice. Surely Kathryn deserved better than his dispassionate appraisal of her death.

"Did you believe her death was an accident?"

"No, there appeared to be a struggle."

"How did you know?"

"Because of the way I found her. She was lying in an irregular position and hurt pretty badly. I knew she'd been attacked."

"Did you call the police?"

"No."

"Did you call for an ambulance?"

"No."

"What *did* you do?"

Reed's jaw tightened. "I don't understand..."

"I mean what did you do next?" Schaeffer stood with both hands tucked in his pockets.

"She was gone. It was too late." Reed brought a shaky hand to his cup and took a sip of water. "I don't remember exactly." He couldn't suppress image of Kathryn's lifeless body. "There was nothing I could do. I held her in my arms. I tried to understand how anyone could do this."

"*Anyone*? You mean *another* person?"

"Yes, *another* person!" Reed looked around for a kind face. One of the jurors swallowed.

Schaeffer was aware that his client was treading water; he knew the next few minutes would be crucial. "What did you do then?"

"I left the house. I needed to get to my car."

"You drove away?"

"No, there was an emergency medical kit in the trunk."

"Did anyone see you when you were outside?"

"Yes, a van drove by and nearly hit me. I'm pretty sure the driver got a good look at my face, but he drove off."

Schaeffer stopped for a moment. "Wait a minute—did you just say an emergency medical kit?" His puzzled look was an honest one. "If Kathryn was dead, why did you need an emergency medical kit?"

Reed searched for the impossible words. "I thought some of her body's cells might still be alive."

Schaeffer wasn't sure where this was going. He was tempted to take a break and find out privately but decided instead to take a chance and let Reed explain. "Please continue."

Robin moved to the edge of her seat. The judge raised his bifocals over the top of his forehead and leaned in. Reed studied the faces in the courtroom, the odd looks of scorn and curiosity, their little porcine eyes squealing for dirt. In Salem they would have cooked him on the spot. He knew there was nothing left to do but tell the truth. "The medical kit contained a sterile swab," he explained. "I used it to collect a sample of tissue from the inside of Kathryn's cheek."

"I see. And what did you intend to do with this tissue?"

"I wanted to place the sample in an incubator to preserve the cells."

"To preserve the cells, of course..." Schaeffer nodded and turned to the jury, inviting them to understand as well. "Did you find an incubator?"

"Yes, my friend had one in his laboratory."

"Who is your friend?"

"Dr. Howell Martin." Reed felt awful saying Howell's name. The most important secrets of his life were unraveling, and there was little he could do about it.

"Why did your friend have an incubator?"

"For the genetic research he was performing, mostly experiments on insects and small animals. He's an expert in somatic cell nuclear transfer, a technique that allows one to remove the DNA from a cell nucleus and insert it into a donor egg."

"For what purpose?"

"To bring the DNA to life—a donor egg infused with DNA can be implanted in a host womb. If properly nourished, the genetic material inside the egg goes through normal cell division. Heart by five weeks, fingers by seven, and so on..."

"Was it your intention to try this experiment on Kathryn's tissue?"

"Yes."

Several jurors began to grin, as if realizing that they'd been the butt of a joke. But Robin wasn't smiling. It was exactly as she'd expected. She turned to Bence Jones and offered a conciliatory nod.

"Dr. Palmer, are you saying that you tried to *clone* Kathryn James?"

Reed took another sip of water. "Yes we tried, but the experiment failed."

A sigh of relief filled the courtroom. The judge sat back in his chair. Schaeffer appeared to exhale as well. It seemed the drama of a murder trial was sufficient for one day.

"Dr. Palmer, your story might explain why you didn't call the police right away, but why even *try* to clone another person? And why Kathryn James?"

All heads turned in Reed's direction. He was certain that none of them, not a single person in the room, would have been worth the sacrifice he made. "I wasn't ready to say goodbye," he said at last. "The shock of discovering Kathryn that way was so horrible, so unacceptable, that I performed a desperate, stupid act. I'm sorry for any confusion it might have caused, but I swear I did not kill Kathryn James."

For the first time, Schaeffer detected a look of compassion in the juror's faces. "No further questions, Your Honor."

The judge turned his attention to Belinda Carver, who was already heading toward the witness box. She glared intensely at Reed. "Doctor Palmer, you have a vivid imagination. I must say that was quite a performance. But really, you can't expect this jury to believe your story."

Reed wasn't sure if he should respond. This was the part that Schaeffer had warned him about, that Carver would corner him with a barrage of closed-ended questions, knowing each answer before he could say a word. "You admit that you were at Kathryn's house on the day of her murder, is that correct?"

"Yes."

"But you didn't tell anyone about it until now?"

"That's correct."

"Your testimony included a man named Dr. Howell Martin. Can you tell us where he is now?"

"No, I cannot."

Carver turned to the judge. "That's because Dr. Howell Martin has disappeared, Your Honor. He failed to respond to our subpoena and nobody knows where he is, not even his family. We think he may be in Mexico." Carver turned back to the witness box. "By the way, was your friend Dr. Martin an accomplice to Kathryn's murder?"

"I doubt it."

"And you're certain that you don't know where he is?"

"I'm afraid not."

"No surprise there," she smiled at the jurors. "Dr. Palmer, you admit that you were in love with the deceased?"

"Yes."

"But she didn't return your love. Is there any reason to believe this didn't upset you?"

"You can believe what you want to."

Carver narrowed her eyes. She moved in the direction of the judge and stopped in front of him. "We've heard several witnesses testify under oath about your volatile behavior and the recent examples of your anger. Do you disagree with any of them?"

"They're entitled to their opinions. I've been upset at times, but I've never hurt anyone." For a moment, Reed's attention was diverted by a man in mechanic's overalls at the rear of the courtroom. When their eyes met, he turned and left the room.

"Your own medical assistant testified under oath that she saw you grab a patient by the throat just a few weeks ago. Is that true?"

"There's no need to exaggerate. I simply held his neck too firmly."

"In an act of rage?"

"I wouldn't call it that."

Carver glanced at the jurors. "Our expert pathologist testified that the cause of Kathryn's death was a broken neck. Show us your hands, Dr. Palmer. Raise them up so everyone can see them."

Schaeffer objected, but the judge allowed it.

"Well?" Carver folded her arms and waited. Reed knew she wanted him to look like a monster in front of everyone. With little choice, he raised his hands into the air. Carver pointed a finger at him. "Your Honor, I can produce witnesses who will testify that Dr. Palmer can crack walnut shells with his bare hands, even rip a telephone book in half." She turned to Reed. "Shall I go on?"

"You can put your hands down," the judge said.

Reed did as he was told and rested a hand on each thigh. "I've only put my hands to good use. You can ask my patients..."

"Right now I'm only interested in the broken neck of a dead woman. Would you have the ability to do this?"

Reed hesitated before walking into another trap. He thought it would have been an opportune time for a loud fire alarm or an earthquake, any excuse to send everyone screaming from the building.

"Answer the question, Dr. Palmer." The judge gave him no choice.

"Yes, I suppose so."

"Of course he did!" Carver turned to the jury. "Not a single person in this room has more knowledge of anatomy or hands as strong. And only Dr. Reed Palmer was at Kathryn James' house on the day of her murder."

Carver turned away from the jury box and punctured every facet of Reed's previous testimony. He was forced to listen as she embellished his presence at the crime scene and the DNA evidence that placed him there. She taunted him with pointed questions about his feelings for Kathryn, cutting down each response with emasculating precision. By the time her closing remarks began, he was but another trophy on her wall.

"Ladies and gentlemen, think whatever you want about Dr. Reed Palmer, because there are no laws to prevent us from *thinking*—no laws designed to govern the fleeting thoughts in our heads, even the random, violent thoughts we might imagine from time to time." She stopped to lift a warning finger. "But think *twice* before your thoughts become actions, because there are laws in place to govern our *actions*—laws that *none* of us is allowed to break, not even the judge."

The judge raised his head.

"Last year, an innocent kindergarten teacher was murdered by the man sitting right here. He violated her in the worst possible way. No, he didn't rape her or dismember her. Far worse, he made her an unwilling partner in a twisted, perverted experiment. When he realized that he couldn't have her on his own terms, he made a sick attempt to *duplicate* her! What a novel solution to rejection—out with the old and in with the new—a plan that could only exist in the mind of a madman.

Carver returned to her desk and retrieved a full-color poster board of enlarged photographs that featured Kathryn as a child, Kathryn as a teenager with her parents, Kathryn teaching her children. The mood of the courtroom turned quiet and nostalgic. Several jurors looked tenderly at one another. Even Kathryn's mother smiled. Then Carver brought out a second poster board of the gruesome photos taken at the murder scene, Kathryn lying on the floor of her home and on the cold steel table of the morgue. Most were full-color close-ups. Robin tugged at the fabric of her pants. Given the chance, most of the people in the room would have strangled Reed right there.

"Ladies and gentlemen, the murder of Kathryn James has shocked our entire community, and you can rest assured that we have found the guilty party responsible for this monstrous act. We have evidence that puts Dr. Reed Palmer squarely at the murder scene. We've heard countless examples of his outbursts of rage and the disturbing confession about his unrequited love for the deceased. Most importantly, we've heard expert testimonies in forensic pathology and psychiatry that support the compelling case against him. After considering this massive burden of evidence, you have no choice but to find Dr. Reed Palmer guilty of murder."

35

Kathryn had believed the concept of atheism was irrelevant to the greater message of love, which is why she made little effort to convince anyone about the presence or absence of a creator. She found no need to complicate matters to get her point across, no need for coercion or illusion. In the classroom or elsewhere, her worldview was similarly straightforward. She promoted respect for the environment and all living things. She believed the time had come to spread a more modern message of inclusion and hope for generations to come.

In terms of politics, there was no party that predefined Kathryn's views. Though many believed that a humanist platform would support a woman's right to choose, there was inertia on the opposite side to be pro-life out of respect for all living things. In matters of gun control there was a plea from many humanists to disarm, while others stood their ground as proud secular Americans who embraced the Second Amendment. Down the line, each partisan view was countered by its opposition—it was simply a matter of perspective—which is why Kathryn was decidedly neutral about such things. In her beloved America, where separation of church and state was promoted by the founding fathers, she considered the role of religion in politics to be moot. Mindful of this, Kathryn's admirers didn't back themselves into a corner by embracing one political party or the other. They hoped instead that the democratic process would prevail and voters would figure out what is right.

* * *

Judge Lambert removed his glasses and pressed a fingertip to each eyelid. His eyeballs felt softer than usual, his skin smooth and dry. He reached for a water pitcher and started to pour as the door opened.

"Your honor, there's a Detective Robin Noel here to see you."

He put his glasses back on. "Let her in."

Robin stepped forward and offered a deferential nod.

"Yes Detective, what do you want?"

The elder judge appeared smaller and less formidable without his black robe, a realization that gave Robin no particular sense of satisfaction. "Your Honor, I'm concerned that the jury hasn't heard the entire story. I believe certain vital information has been suppressed."

"Which information are you referring to?"

"The genetic experiment sir. I'm not entirely convinced that it failed."

The judge took a step past Robin to close the chamber door. He hesitated on his way back to his desk to estimate her purpose. "On what do you base your suspicion?"

"Let's say it's a hunch."

"I see." He showed no sign of agreement, though he was intrigued by Robin's intuition. "I appreciate your opinion, Detective. Is there anything else?"

"Yes, sir," she persisted. "What if the experiment didn't fail? Don't you think it would be important to know?"

"Important to know what, Detective? Like it or not, the answer won't change the fact that your friend was killed." He saw Robin squinting and could not tell if it reflected anger or annoyance. In his younger days he might have chastised her for looking at him that way.

"Friendship has nothing to do with it," she said. "I'm trying to solve a crime and get justice here. I want the jury to hear all the relevant information, don't you?"

"Detective, I regret the loss of your friend, but I don't want to hear any more about this." The judge placed a hand over the small of his back and winced as he sat down.

Robin checked her watch and realized that she was running late. With a cordial goodbye, she backpedaled to the door and let herself out. Upon her return to the precinct, she was informed that a man had been waiting for her. Robin found him sitting at her desk, for how long she could not say. She studied his face and knew that he looked familiar. Dressed in mechanic's overalls, he appeared hardened on the surface, with sorrowful eyes that looked away. A scar showed at the corner of each brow, a tattoo at the side of his neck. His knuckles were calloused and darkened, an index finger stained by tobacco.

"Who are you?" she asked.

"Billy Carlyle," he said.

"What do you want?"

"The kindergarten teacher—I saw her on the morning she was killed." He smiled weakly.

"Where did you see her?"

"I was with two other guys that day. One of them named Ramsey works at a gas station upstate." The uttering of Ramsey's name seemed to bother him. "We saw her at the library."

Robin calmly asked, "Did one of your friends kill Kathryn James?"

"No way. I didn't say that." Billy held tight to his seat. "She came out of the library and bumped into Ramsay. It was just an accident, but he's crazy as hell. I thought we were all going to get arrested that day. It was all over the news, everybody asking questions…"

Robin held her tongue and let him continue.

"Her car was right there. She got in and drove away. So we jumped into Ramsay's van and followed her. Around ten minutes later, she got to her house and walked inside. We drove around her block a few times talking about how we were going to knock on her door or something…"

"Where did you come from? I saw you in the courtroom the other day."

Billy nodded.

"Who's putting you up to this?"

"Nobody… look, I didn't have to come here. Ramsay would kill me if he knew I was talking to you." Billy moved to the edge of his chair and got ready to leave.

"Alright, so what happened? What did you do to Kathryn?"

"Like I told you, we were just fooling around, that's all. We drove around the block a few times, and when we got back to her house we saw this guy come running out the front door. He's the one who did it, we all knew right away. We didn't like the look of it so we got out of there."

"You saw someone? Who was it?" Robin demanded.

"The guy who sits at the front of the courtroom..."

Robin pounded a fist on the table. "I *knew* it!

"Not the doctor, the guy who sits next to you."

"Wait a minute, you mean next to me in the courtroom?" Robin had to catch her breath. "Are you sure about this? Did your friend Ramsay see him too?"

"You'd have to ask him," Billy said. "One more thing, around an hour later we cruised back to the house, and that's when we saw the doctor step off the porch. He looked scared, like he had to get somewhere fast. He crossed the street and almost walked right into the van."

Robin leaned closer. "Let me get this straight: you think the first man you saw at Kathryn's house was the one who killed her?"

"Yeah, we were all pretty sure."

"Not the doctor?"

"That's right. I won't have to testify, will I?"

"Probably not. The trial is over," Robin said. "The defense has rested and the jury's been sequestered."

"So I can go?"

Robin had no grounds to keep him there. She took his phone number and let him go. "Son of a bitch," she muttered.

DiPalma had been listening from his desk. "That's heavy shit," he said. "So what are you going to do now?"

Robin knew right away. "I think I'll have a little chat with our friend, the assistant DA."

* * *

The sun seemed to take forever to rise. With the verdict only minutes away, Bence Jones kept a watchful eye on the empty jury box. "What's taking them so long?"

Robin sat in her usual spot next to him. "Maybe it wasn't an open and shut case after all."

"You're kidding, right?"

"I'm serious. You never know what the jurors are saying behind closed doors. I mean, it's hard to get twelve people to agree on anything, let alone a guilty verdict." She watched him carefully. "But I think Carver managed to pull it off."

"I certainly hope so." Bence rose from his seat and stepped into the aisle.

"Where are you going?"

"To the men's room..."

Robin's imposing gaze kept him in place. "Before you go, I have a question. What do you know about a man named D'Ante Boyd?"

Bence drew his legs together. "I don't recognize the name."

She waited. "What's the matter?"

"Nothing's the matter. I just want this thing over with." He leaned into the aisle, unsure if he could go.

Robin kept her eyes focused squarely on him as if he were tethered to a leash. Her cell phone vibrated and she didn't budge. She maintained a look of vigilance for a few seconds before taking the call. She learned that a visitor named Brenda Jones had arrived at the precinct with a DVD. "Okay thanks. I'll be there in an hour." She turned back to Bence and said, "I'm curious to know why you did it."

"Did what?" His voice cracked.

"Call me. You could have called anyone that day. What made you think I'd have an interest in this case?"

"You and Kathryn were friends."

Robin sensed his growing discomfort. Ordinarily she would have pecked away at the surface until he caved, but time was running out.

Bodies began to fill the seats around them. Bence nodded to a fellow parishioner in the next row. "Some gratitude," he whispered. "What's with the third degree?"

"I don't know what you're talking about."

Bence noticed that a line of jurors was entering the courtroom. "I might as well wait," he said, finding his seat again.

Robin watched him cross his legs. She enjoyed this kind of advantage during tense interrogations, but with the verdict only moments away, she felt a sense of urgency. "By the way, do you remember where Kathryn lived?"

"Yes, of course."

"Have you ever been to her house?"

"Sure."

She leaned in more closely. "How about on the day she was killed?"

Bence dismissed the question as if it hadn't even been asked. The courtroom grew unbearably noisy around them and Robin had difficulty interpreting his muted response. Perhaps he hadn't even heard the question.

Reed and Schaeffer waited at the defense table. The judge ascended to the bench and all were asked to rise. Reed looked at the faces of the jurors and made eye contact with a benevolent looking lady. She returned a hopeful smile. The judge uttered a few words about the decorum of his courtroom for those who might disagree with the jury's decision. Satisfied that his message was properly received, he signaled to the foreman. "Will the defendant please stand."

Reed did as he was told. Schaeffer stood as well.

"Do you have anything to say before the verdict is announced?"

"Yes, Your Honor, I'd like to say something." This was the part of the process that Reed abhorred most of all. Considering the porous evidence against him, he knew it should have been easy to convince this jury of his innocence, though he sensed the atmosphere of the courtroom was hostile by any estimation and feared the verdict was already a fait accompli. He turned to face the jury. "Ladies and gentlemen, I am standing in front of you with my life hanging in the balance, not begging for mercy, but simply asking you to have faith in a fellow human being. If you are wondering what I have done to deserve your faith, the answer is simply that I am a fellow human being worthy of the same fair treatment you'd expect for yourselves.

"For years I've given my patients the attention they needed and wanted, which means equal attention, and that's what I'm asking of you now: the fairness you would hope for in my position. I'm asking you to have faith in me. It's what Kathryn would have wanted. If you can accept that having faith in me will lead to the truth, then you'll understand what Kathryn was trying to express in her writings, that when you help a fellow person in need, you realize how important you are and how much influence you truly have. No miracle is required to save an innocent man from being punished for a crime he didn't commit. All you need is an honest assessment of what happened on the day of Kathryn's death.

"Kathryn once said *faith is what we allow ourselves to believe.* If she were here right now, she would remind us that the literal definition of faith is *belief that is not based on proof.* Well, the law inside a courtroom requires something more than faith—the law requires *proof regardless of faith*—and this makes a juror's task less complicated. The requirement of proof sets a jury free from the frailty of human error. If there is insufficient evidence, as is the case in this trial, the proper verdict is *innocent.*" Reed turned to the judge. "And I am innocent. Thank you, Your Honor."

The judge turned to the jury box. "What is your verdict?"

The foreman stood and unfolded a single piece of paper. "For the murder of Kathryn James, we find the defendant Dr. Reed Palmer *guilty.*"

Reed had no immediate reaction. Overwhelmed by noise and confusion, the word *guilty* bounced around his head searching for meaning. The foreman stared intensely at Reed to show him that the jury had made the correct decision. Bence Jones looked up at the heavens with clenched fists to punctuate his response. Carver and her team shook hands to congratulate each other. Schaeffer shook his head in frustration and customarily closed his briefcase. The judge expressed his own disappointment by firmly striking his gavel.

Before Reed knew what was happening, he was grabbed above the elbow and ushered out of the courtroom by the secure grip of the bailiff. He couldn't make out the exact words and taunts hurled in his direction, though he had a fairly good idea. One spectator, a parishioner from the Church of God, managed to get in a good kick to the shin. That bothered him most of all.

PART 4

The Tribulations

36

Reed's holding cell was a welcome reprieve from the madness of the courtroom—but he had already learned that time moves slowly when there is nothing to do, and since the next stop was going to be a lengthy incarceration, it seemed that Robin's appearance brought an unlikely sense of relief. Anything to delay the inevitable was fine, as far as Reed was concerned.

Robin dragged a stool toward the bars and kept her place on the opposite side. "You'll be transferred to a federal prison in a few hours."

"Yes, I know."

"I spoke to a man who said he saw you leaving Kathryn's house on the day of her murder."

"In case you've forgotten, I made no secret about being there."

"Just listen to me for a minute." Her expression suggested friendly concern. "He was a passenger in the white van described in your testimony. His name is Billy Carlyle, a mechanic. Do you know him?"

"No." Reed approached the bars. "Is that all you wanted?"

"Right now all I want is the truth."

"*Now* you want the truth?"

"That's all I ever wanted," she said without a trace of apology. "I must admit, I was surprised when your attorney asked you to take the stand."

"Actually, it was *my* idea. I wanted to tell my side of the story."

"Well, it was a mistake." She pushed herself off the stool and began to pace. "I've seen my share of criminals over the years, but there's something different about you Palmer. I mean, you're friendly enough on the surface—like you have nothing to hide, but you never really divulge much about yourself, do you?" She waited for a response then began to pace once more. "And why should I care? A guilty verdict puts an end to it all, right?"

"What do you want from me?"

She looked directly at him. "I want to know what really happened that day."

"What really happened? That's what you want to know?"

"Well?"

Reed discovered for the first time that he actually liked Robin. The concern in her voice reflected not only a real commitment to justice but her affection for Kathryn. "This wasn't just another case for you, Detective. It was something more, wasn't it?"

"I'm asking the questions."

Reed sensed a change in her attitude, something he couldn't quite define. "You must think we're completely different," he said, "the cop and the criminal on either side of these bars—but there is one thing we do have in common."

"I doubt it. What could you and I possibly have in common?"

"How about Kathryn?" Reed drew closer to the bars until their faces were only inches apart. "Think about it Robin, you know how much I loved her, and your presence here is proof."

"Proof of what?" she asked.

"That you loved her too."

Without warning, Robin reached through the bars and grabbed Reed by the collar. He fell forward and struck his right cheek against the bars. They shared a moment of weird intimacy as their faces were forcibly pressed together, their mouths breathing heavily into one another's. Finally she unclenched her fists and shoved Reed away. "I don't care about your feelings for Kathryn. And my personal feelings are none of your business."

Reed's cheek throbbed where it had struck the bars. "Sorry I brought it up." He touched the side of his face to see if he was bleeding.

"Sorry or not," she said, tucking in a loose shirttail, "I want the right person punished."

"You'll get no argument from me." He smiled hopefully.

She dragged the stool back to the edge of the cell. "That's why I'm here. I have some information that might be useful."

"But the trial is over."

"Yes, but my investigation isn't."

* * *

The neighborhood was still abuzz when Robin packed an overnight bag and took a long drive upstate to a sleepy town called Mooresville. Barely visible on the map, it had once boasted a thriving cannery and a rubber-band factory. Since then, Mooresville was defined by little more than a roadside diner, a chapel and a full-service gas station. After a three-hour drive, Robin rolled off the Interstate and pulled up to a gas pump. She turned off the engine and waited.

The brief silence was a welcome departure from the precinct. Robin typically grew restless in a quiet rural area where there wasn't much for a city detective to do. As she waited for the gas station attendant, it occurred to her that it might not be so terrible to settle down in a place like this. With Ramsay's appearance in mind, she noticed a bearded man with a baseball cap emerge from the minimart. This was followed by the sound of a gas nozzle entering the side of her car with a clunk. From her side-view mirror, she saw the attendant slouch against the car with his face turned upward to the sun.

She cleared her throat and asked, "Is this Mooresville?"

"Yes, ma'am..."

"I'm looking for someone. Maybe you can help me."

"I know everyone," he winked.

"How about Ramsay Hunt?"

"You're looking at him."

Robin's pulse quickened. She instinctively brought a hand to the holster beneath her left armpit, unfastened its snap and looked down once more at the photo beside the console. The beard was new. As she lifted the wallet-sized photo to get a better look, a shadow fell over her. Ramsay reached into the car and took the photo from her hand. "Well, well," he said, inspecting it. He handed the photo back to Robin and returned his attention to the pump.

Robin exhaled. He didn't seem quite as crazy as Billy had described. "You must be wondering why I'm looking for you."

"No, I figured somebody would come by sooner or later."

"Why?"

"To ask about the girl." He topped off the gas and replaced the cap. "Did you talk to Billy yet?"

"Yes, I did. He told me where to find you."

Ramsay smiled at the thought. "That'll be thirty for the gas. You can park the car over there and come inside."

Robin drove several yards past the pumps to a stretch of gravel, where she texted DiPalma of her whereabouts, just in case, then patted her holster and walked to the mini-mart. No patrons were around. She leaned forward against the countertop and studied Ramsay's face. "You saw the verdict on the news?"

"Yep."

"Was the right man convicted for the murder?"

"Nope."

"How do you know?"

"Just one of those things. Billy must've told you, we followed that girl home from the library. We were bored I guess, just having a little fun. Nobody was going to get hurt. Anyway, a few minutes after she got home we saw this guy come out of her house. He's the one who did it, we knew as soon as the news hit."

Robin placed a group of six photographs on the counter in front of him. "Do you recognize him in any of these?"

Ramsay picked one of the photos and flicked it in Robin's direction.

"Would you be willing to testify?"

He surveyed his surroundings. "If you put me up at a nice hotel, I will. Besides, it'll give me a chance to see Billy again. I have a few things to get off my chest."

"I'm not sure that he's too anxious to see you."

"That's why I want to see him, to show him that I'm really not so bad after all."

"Good." Robin gathered the photos and left a pair of twenties on the counter. "I'll let you know when we're ready. It might take a while to arrange a meeting with the judge, but I'll be in touch."

"I'm not going anywhere."

Robin returned to her car and texted DiPalma again. As she drove off, Ramsay leaned against a gas pump and watched the familiar dust rise from the road.

37

During the first few weeks of his incarceration, Reed stayed inside his cell as much as possible. He figured it was the safest place to be. Then he realized the cells were left open and unsupervised during morning break, leaving him vulnerable to roving gangs. That's when he got into the habit of joining the other inmates outside in the courtyard under the purview of the guards.

A month into his sentence, an unsettling noise drew his attention, a muffled commotion that seemed innocent at first and more ominous as he approached. He soon realized what was happening. A circle of men had walled off the hazing of an inmate while five others held him down.

Reed's first impulse was to rush in and help the overmatched man, though he knew the more prudent choice was to run in the opposite direction and tell one of the guards. In either case, to simply ignore the attack was not an option. He figured whatever evil that inmate did to earn his place in jail would not justify his being tortured that way. Against his better judgment, Reed leaned into the wall of inmates and got ready to break through when a strong hand pulled him back.

"Where do you think you're going, Doc?"

Reed looked up at the huge inmate, who was nearly a head taller. "I'm going to help that man."

"No, you're not." He held Reed by the upper arm and guided him away.

The struggle inside the circle of men seemed to intensify even as they drew further from it. "You can let go of me now," Reed appealed with a shake of the arm, but he could not break free. "They're going to kill that guy and you know it."

"What I know, Doc, is that you were about to make a big mistake."

Until then, nobody in prison had referred to Reed as *Doc*. That's when he remembered the inmate's face, a former patient who'd strained his back lifting merchandise off a parked truck. They both grinned at the irony of meeting in jail. "What was it, furniture?"

"Televisions," he let go of Reed's arm. "You're not going to kill me too, are you?"

The immediate joke was that Reed was no match for the larger man, but the hidden message was unmistakable. "You think I killed that woman?"

"No, Doc."

Reed felt exonerated for the first time in months. "Well, I didn't."

"I know you didn't."

Reed treaded carefully here. He considered the code among inmates with little desire for small talk. Ask a question and you might get an answer. Every now and then a colorful storyteller would come through and keep everyone entertained at his own peril. Pride was in abundance and inmates were easily offended for reasons that were not entirely clear. More than a few loudmouths had to be carted away. It was the first lesson that Reed had learned behind bars: to mind his own business. "Are you saying you know who did it?"

"No, I just know it wasn't you."

The words that nobody will ever hear, Reed thought. "How do you know it wasn't me?"

"A friend on the outside said they got the wrong guy."

Reed swallowed hard. "Does he know who did it?"

"Even if he did, nobody would listen. He's a convict like you and me."

The courtyard turned strangely quiet. The circle of men had dispersed without a trace of incident. "I suppose you're right."

"Now, you want to tell me what you had in mind back there, Doc?"

"That man needed help. He could have been raped or killed."

"Which one, raped or killed?"

"Does it matter?"

"It didn't matter to him. On the outside he did both. Do you know why he's in here?"

"You're going to tell me that he's a rapist and a murderer so it's okay that he gets fucked and tortured in prison, right?"

"No, I'm just suggesting," the imposing inmate rested a heavy finger on Reed's chest, "that you think about *yourself* next time. Because the next time you try something stupid like that again, I won't be here to pull you back, you got it?" He stared Reed up and down. "I'm not here to be your guardian angel. I'm getting out next week."

"Thanks, I'll try to remember that." Reed felt the full impact of his sentence. He was in it for the long haul and just getting started.

*   *   *

In a suburb of Ohio, a priest and a nun who had served together for five years made headlines when they announced their love for one another. A good friend became a Universal Life minister and performed the wedding ceremony. The former priest exchanged his collar for wedding band and the former nun became pregnant with their first child. With Kathryn's writings in mind, they forged a humanist congregation that became the most popular in town. A rally of donations enabled them to erect a robust structure of natural stone, a pipe organ to accompany its lively choir, an after-school youth program, and a thriving community daycare center. People visited out of curiosity at first and many called it their new spiritual home. The mainstream secular values imparted by the loving couple were inspirational to all who entered.

When word of their experience had spread to neighboring towns, similar congregations sprouted up everywhere. What began as a sparse collection of pins on the map spread to the coasts and beyond. It was then decided, with no shortage of debate, that a proper name for Kathryn's belief system was missing—a shorthand or nosology of sorts to help identify the movement, but without labeling it as *religion*, per se. This spurred further controversy about what religion actually is, and it was ultimately determined that *A Religion Called Love* qualified as a new religion after all. Once that was settled, people were happy to say the words that Kathryn would have enjoyed: *my religion is love.*

*   *   *

In the months prior to her death, Kathryn regularly attended Sunday Assembly, where her love of nature and humanity were often validated (or challenged in some cases). In the months after her death, these grass-roots gatherings spread through social media to venues that were more acoustically sound. People attended on a weekly basis to celebrate life, plan charitable events, and sing songs that were spiritually uplifting and secular in nature—songs such as "Imagine," "Peace Train," "Love Train," "This Land Is Your Land," "What's So Funny About Peace Love and Understanding," with a vibe of communal joy reminiscent of the lively church services that Kathryn had attended as a child. The sporadic references to *God* within the lyrics were casually interpreted as *love* or *goodness*, a whimsical view consistent with Kathryn's own. The musings posed in her manuscript were nothing new—she'd borrowed from those whose progressive values served as a foundation for progress—and if she built upon the legacy of others, wasn't that the point of inspiration?

Along the way, a special person stepped forward to join the movement: Father Francis, the former priest, fully sober and attentive to Kathryn's original intentions, spoke persuasively on her behalf and charmed audiences with his colorful recollections of their shared world view. When his older brother John came to his side, the inertia that followed was nothing short of astounding. *A Religion called Love* was celebrated by those who felt the terms religion and love belonged to everyone. The peace sign, once a badge of nuclear disarmament became an adopted emblem for the movement, calling further attention to the importance of world peace. The progressive agenda wove itself into the fabric of society where military-style assault weapons were summarily banned, the death penalty was abolished, prisons released all non-violent criminals, and a renewed emphasis on education and the environment created exciting new opportunities for all.

As a man believes, so he will act

-Sam Harris

38

After the guilty verdict, assistant DA Bence Jones spent an inordinate amount of time in his office. A black leather swivel chair by the window enabled him to keep a bird's eye view on the parking lot. He had a suspicion that sooner or later Robin would come, and when she finally did, he felt a strange sense of relief. From his perch on the third floor, he watched her get out of her car and disappear under the façade of the main entrance. Now it was just a matter of time.

He swiveled around and rested both hands on his desk, secure in the knowledge that all visitors entering the prosecutor's wing had to stop at a safety check point and surrender all weapons before passing through. His top desk drawer contained a roll of breath mints, a black comb and a loaded pistol.

Robin was directed to Bence's office. Once inside, she closed the door and carefully approached.

Bence leaned over his papers, feigning work. "I'm a little busy here."

Her intuition was on fire. She couldn't explain why, but Kathryn's presence was everywhere. It was a curious sensation for Robin, who had always doubted the possibility of such things. "I need to discuss something important with you about the trial."

"What is there to discuss?"

"Two men are prepared to testify that you were at Kathryn's house on the day she was killed."

"So?"

"You never said anything about it."

"There was nothing to say." Bence steadied his breathing under Robin's watchful eye. She couldn't tell if it reflected innocence or deceit.

"What do you know about a man named D'Ante Boyd?"

"Never heard of him."

She measured each response carefully, and he studied her with equal scrutiny. Each had a healthy suspicion of the other, their preconceived judgments obliterating any fair assessment. Bence casually reached into his desktop drawer and produced the loaded pistol. Robin flinched in the direction of her empty holster.

Bence held the gun at eye level and looked at it with admiration. "It belonged to my father."

"May I see it?" Robin extended an opened hand. She gulped imperceptibly.

To her surprise, Bence reached across the desk and offered the weapon. "It's a beauty, isn't it?"

Accepting it, she inspected its markings and shared his approval. She felt the weight of its mass in her palm and estimated that it was loaded. Confident now that she was only inches from Kathryn's killer, she considered the likelihood that only one of them would walk away alive.

Bence held a palm out and gestured for Robin to return the weapon. Rather than hand it back to him, she placed it on the desk directly between them. Bence found the possibilities intriguing.

Her impetuous act restored balance to their discussion. They stared blankly at one another, their mutual line of vision only several inches above the loaded weapon.

"I have to tell you," Robin said, "New questions are being raised about the verdict."

"What kind of questions?"

"Like who really killed Kathryn..."

A distant look surfaced on Bence's face. His thoughts drifted to Kathryn's bedroom on the day of her murder. It was Saturday morning; she was at the library and would not be home for a while. He sorted through her chest of drawers for personal items and read several passages of her private journal that held his interest for a while. He found a bulky spiraled photo album and leafed through its thick cardboard pages, looking specifically for photos that featured Kathryn. He selected one and tucked it into his shirt pocket. Setting the album aside, he fell back onto Kathryn's unmade bed, where the crumpled sheets smelled just like her. He buried his face into her pillow then turned his head and noticed a pile of clothing on the floor, a pajama shirt and a pair of panties. He tried to estimate how long it had been since Kathryn had last worn them.

Without warning, the unmistakable sound of footsteps on the front porch was followed by a jiggling of keys. Bence jumped from the bed, took a step toward the closet and chose instead to rush down the hallway to the bathroom. He climbed into a shower tub and drew the curtain halfway. In the interminable silence that followed, he kept himself well hidden.

The front door opened and closed with a thud. The muffled sound of footsteps on carpet grew closer, then more distant until there was no sound at all. After a minute of waiting, Bence brought a hand up to the shower curtain and got ready to make a break for the door when the bathroom light snapped on.

A dizzying pulse of blood rushed past his ears. Kathryn stepped past the shower curtain to the toilet and unzipped her jeans. The familiar tinkling sound gave Bence a chance to breathe unheard. He caught a glimpse of her from the shadows as she wiped herself and washed her hands. Finally, she returned past the shower curtain and shut the light. Taking no further chances, Bence remained hidden for another ten minutes before attempting to leave. When he felt the time was right, he stepped out of the tub, poked his head into the hallway to make sure the coast was clear, and tiptoed to the front door.

"Who's there?"

Bence stopped in his tracks. Too late to make a run for it, he turned to face Kathryn.

"What are you doing here?" she demanded.

"I rang the doorbell." He pointed a thumb over his shoulder. "The door was open."

Kathryn looked at the door. "It was not! Get out of here!" She shoved Bence in the chest. "What are you doing? Let go of me!"

"Well?" Robin waited for his answer.

The assistant DA lowered his palms onto the table. As if daring her to draw first, he didn't move until she did. A presence flooded the room. A shot rang out. Bence's secretary rushed in and screamed at the sight of Robin's bloodied face.

Robin staggered past the startled woman. Several feet away, Bence was slumped forward over his desk, a bullet lodged in his brain. The gun rested on the desk in front of him.

Robin reached into her pocket and removed a white handkerchief. With a shaky hand, she wiped the blood from her face and punched a number into her cell phone. "Yes, this is Detective Robin Noel. I'd like to report a suicide."

39

At the edge of the courtyard, beside the free weights, a husky inmate dangled his arm and wagged it about in pendulum-like fashion. "I had pain there for two years and you got rid of it in two minutes. How the fuck did you do that?"

"A little trick I learned," Reed said. A jagged scar over the inmate's serratus posterior band had irritated a subcostal nerve. A simple adjustment was all he needed.

"Man that feels better." He rotated his torso from left to right. "I owe you, man. What do you need, cigarettes?"

"Don't mention it." Reed allowed a moment of satisfaction. He looked up into the late morning sky and imagined Shirley standing on the patio with a cigarette right about now. She would have accepted the inmate's offer, but the office was closed and the lights were off. Reed had just started to walk away when a strong arm reached out and held him in place.

"Where the fuck are you going?"

"I said we're even. Don't mention it."

"I said cigarettes!! Don't turn your back on me, mother fucker." He shoved Reed aside and walked past with an ape-like, muscle-bound stride, as if he were carrying a bulky parcel under each arm. Reed was left wondering how close he had come to getting impaled, or worse. For the rest of the morning, he stayed in a highly visible area under the purview of the guards. He waited for the sun to creep past the guard tower and cast a shadow at the base of the courtyard fence, which usually meant fifteen more minutes until lunch. When the moment arrived, he braced for the loud bell. The first few times shook him out of his skin.

"Palmer!" a voice shouted from behind. "You have a visitor."

Reed followed the prison guard to central processing, where he found Robin leaning over a desktop, filling out several forms. Her hair was longer than he had last remembered. The reading glasses were new. She didn't smile upon seeing him, though she didn't seem unhappy either. "Your release papers," she said, returning her attention to the task in front of her. The forms had already been signed by Judge Lambert and Attorney Schaeffer. In light of all that had happened, Reed had been granted a new trial.

"You didn't have to do this for me, Robin. I could've taken a cab."

She signed the last of the forms and clicked her pen. "Let's just say I have few connections to Kathryn and you happen to be one of them."

"More than just a connection," Reed said. "We both loved her."

For the first time, Robin allowed a tiny smile to break through, an unforced lovely smile. But something was left unresolved; it showed in her eyes.

"What's wrong?"

She shook her head. "You loved Kathryn, I loved Kathryn, everyone loved her—but I wonder if she ever really loved any of us."

"You're kidding, right?"

"I'm afraid not," Robin said. "I wanted her in the worst way, more than you'll ever know. I must admit though, when we finally got to spend time together, I discovered something unexpected. She had a great capacity to love and she talked a lot about love, but on an intimate level there was something untouchable about her. Unreachable, you know? Or maybe it was just me." For a few seconds Robin appeared vulnerable, waiting for Reed to corroborate. "Have you ever noticed that about her?"

"She loved teaching kids," he said. "Maybe that was enough."

"The two of you never..."

"Kathryn and me? No." Reed smiled at the thought. "And you?"

"Not even close." Robin shook her head. "The funny thing is: the more I wanted her, the more she left me wanting. Does that make sense? It's like the challenge was to break through that protective wall of hers, to conquer her indifference."

"Kathryn was hardly indifferent. You saw her writings; she cared more about people than anyone I've ever known, and here we are criticizing her for not wanting us, licking our wounds, lamenting our failure to win her affection. What do you think she'd say about that? I mean, at some point we need to realize that *love* is not only about us. She understood that a lot better than we do."

An armed guard brought them to the cellblocks, where Reed was allowed to claim a few personal items and stuff them into a duffle bag. "You know I received a few letters from Mallory. It sounds like she's doing well."

Robin let her guard down once more. "Yeah, she's doing great, no pain at all. I know she'd like to thank you in person."

Reed was glad to hear it. "By the way, how did you get the judge to expedite the hearing?"

"He said you can thank an old poker buddy of his."

Reed made the connection right away. He had to grin at the thought of Jake Krauss playing poker with Judge Lambert. That old crouton of a cabbie was right every time. Stepping back outside the bars, Reed looked down at the stripped-down cot for the last time and pitied the poor soul coming to take his place. A wave of emotion consumed him. The horrible noises and smells, the constant threats of violence, none of it would be forgotten, but he would surely leave it.

They returned through the corridors to central processing, where the sounds of prison echoed all around. When they arrived at the main prison gates, Reed took a moment to drop his duffle bag to the ground. He looked up and felt the sun on his face. Robin stood by and allowed him to soak up the sensation, the kind of boundless space only a free person can know. Reed knew it was the same sunshine he had seen a thousand times from inside the prison walls, except it felt different now. Or perhaps his point of view had changed. So often he had witnessed a metamorphosis in the lives of others, a transformation that seemed impossible had they not ushered it in themselves. Kathryn had once tried to explain the phenomenon to him, and now he understood.

He picked up his duffle bag and followed Robin through the parking lot. When they neared her car, she slowed and lagged behind, as if holding something back.

"What's the matter?"

"The experiment," she said.

"Which experiment?"

"You know what I mean."

Reed did not want to discuss any part of it. "I told you, the experiment failed."

Robin waited for more. She wanted Reed to admit that the experiment was a success, not only to satisfy her stubborn desire to be correct, but for the same reason the experiment was performed in the first place, to preserve a part of Kathryn. But there would be no confession, so they resumed their stoll to Robin's car, where she stared across the roof, opened the door locks, and got in with no further discussion about Howell or the experiment. Reed suspected that she was too smart to be lured elsewhere, so he didn't bother trying. He reached over his shoulder, pulled the seatbelt across and clicked.

They drove off with the windows rolled down, sidestepping any discussion about the trial or Kathryn. They shared a few superficial observations about life in general, including Reed's sneaking desire to stop at Roll 'n Roaster for a roast beef sandwich with melted cheese. Robin laughed because she had eaten there just the other day. Minutes later she turned onto Reed's block, where she pulled up to the curb of his house and left the motor running. There was no fanfare upon his arrival, no welcome reception or any yellow ribbons.

"You want to come in?"

"No thanks." She maintained a look of vigilance.

"Tell me the truth Robin, why did you bring me here? You didn't have to."

She shrugged. "Call me crazy, but Bence Jones never actually confessed. I might have to keep an eye on you for a while."

"I hope you're kidding."

She didn't answer.

Reed stepped out of the car and watched Robin drive off. With the duffle bag over his shoulder, he looked up and saw that his house had fallen into serious disrepair. A few friends and neighbors had pitched in along the way to maintain the front lawn, but there was still much work to be done. Most of the windows had been broken. A slur written across the front door in red spray paint had been partially scrubbed off, though its meaning was clear enough. Flapping in the breeze, stuck in a thorn bush by the porch, was a twisted remnant of yellow police tape. His yellow ribbon.

40

Tina had agreed to join Reed for a drive on this special day, the anniversary of Kathryn's death. The teenager knew little about Kathryn James other than the rumors from many years earlier. Every now and then a neighbor would make a comment about Tina's appearance and her uncanny resemblance to the pretty kindergarten teacher who was killed years earlier.

Reed sensed something strange in the air between them. He wondered if Penny had told her something. As if tuned to his thoughts, Tina posed a question. "Are you my father?"

He gripped the steering wheel a bit tighter. "No sweetheart."

"Yes, you are." She grinned as if knowing a secret.

He turned to look at her. The similarity to Kathryn triggered a wave of melancholy. It never failed to amaze him. He pulled over to the side of the road and shut the engine off. "You can think of me as your father if you like, but as far as your biological father is concerned… well, maybe your mother should tell you."

"I think she's waiting for the right time. Anyway, I thought it might be you."

"I'm afraid not."

Tina wasn't sure if she should be relieved or disappointed. "So if you're not my father then who is?"

"Some people never find out." Reed was bursting to say more. He and Penny had privately discussed the matter on several occasions and agreed to wait until Tina turned sixteen. He started the car once more and drove off. "I noticed that you didn't ask me about your mother. Have you ever wondered about her?"

"What's there to ask? She described every detail about her labor and delivery on the day I was born. I know for a *fact* that she's my real mother."

"Yes, Penny is your real mother and she raised you beautifully." A lump expanded in Reed's throat. "But today we're going to visit someone else."

"What are you talking about?"

Reed kept his eyes on the road ahead. "It's difficult to explain. That's why I'm taking you to a place where I can show you."

"Show me what?" Tina's voice tightened. "Do we really have to do this today?"

"Trust me, it's alright." Reed turned onto a private drive that led to the arches of a cemetery. Slowing to a crawl, they followed a line of flat shrubs that led to a stone building and a nicely landscaped lawn with hundreds of headstones extending outward to the horizon. Reed's car moved through the narrow lanes like a canoe on still water, past a gathering of mourners that briefly looked up. Tina held her breath with a sense of relief as the car passed them without stopping. A patch of clouds drifted across the sky. A rabbit poked its head up from behind a rock. Then a familiar landmark came into view, a pair of twisted white birches beside a weeping willow. Reed pulled over and asked Tina to wait. "This won't take long."

He stepped into a manicured garden of Junipers and Hibiscus. At the center was Kathryn's headstone. A bunch of wildflowers sat beneath her name. Emerald blades of grass swirled about, her essence swirling into the breeze. Reed lowered his head and surrendered himself to the moment, imagining the life that Kathryn might have had, the children she could have taught, and the happiness they might have shared. With moist eyes, he remained kneeling for another minute, then brushed himself off and returned to the car.

As he approached the passenger window, he saw Tina's face superimposed on his own reflection. He opened the car door and took Tina by the hand.

"Where are we going?"

"To meet someone..."

Tina followed Reed to Kathryn's gravesite, where he explained everything about the drama of his friendship with Kathryn, the mystery of Penny's pregnancy, the details of his arrest and the trial that followed. Tina wasn't the least bit upset to learn about Howell's experiment. Quite the opposite, she was fascinated to learn about her miraculous conception and the unique DNA that swirled within her. Reed made sure to emphasize Penny's courage and sacrifice during their time of desperate need. When he pointed out the significance of Kathryn's enlightened beliefs and the importance of her manuscript, he was delighted to learn that Tina, like millions of others, had already embraced her secular yet spiritual views.

Their visit complete, they returned through the narrow lanes of the cemetery to the streets of the real world, where reason matters more than rhetoric, and acts of kindness matter more than words.

ABOUT THE AUTHOR:

David Trock has written in several genres, notably non-fiction in the field of medicine. His book, "Healing Fibromyalgia," provided insight into a common source of chronic pain. His book chapters and journal articles have been widely published. Dr. Trock's interest in the human mind has motivated him to write the novel, A Religion Called Love—a modern exploration of the limits of behavior and the lasting impact of choices made by ordinary people. He is married with two grown children and lives in Connecticut.